JOU

I smiled in an attempt to reassure her that my intentions were as honourable as might be expected. But it seemed to me that she was more amused than shocked, and I took new heart.

I tried to rise, quite forgetting that my hand was still half a yard up her skirt, and succeeded only in tumbling half a'top of her, my left hand accidentally landing on her swelling bubbies.

Where I stabbed my finger on the pin of a brooch of amethysts and opals that held the bodice together.

"Ouch!"

"Poor boy. What's wrong now?"

My tongue has a sad habit, at times of great emotion, of becoming tangled up with my mind, so that the words that leave my brain never reach my mouth in the same order.

"I fear that you have pricked my finger."

That was what I intended to say.

My sense of delicacy forbids me to mention the words that I heard my tongue utter, though I suspect that the more frank-minded among you might make a shrewd guess.

And it was at this moment, overhearing my words, that her escort finally found her.

And me...

Journal of a Young Rake

Tom Goane

edited by
Christopher Nolan

CORONET BOOKS
Hodder and Stoughton

Copyright © Christopher Nolan, 1976

First published in Great Britain 1977 by
Coronet Books

Printed in Great Britain for
Hodder and Stoughton Paperbacks, a
division of Hodder and Stoughton Ltd.,
Mill Road, Dunton Green, Sevenoaks, Kent
by Hazell Watson & Viney Ltd,
Aylesbury, Bucks

ISBN 0 340 21569 0

This is for Chris, with thanks

"Forth, to the alien gravity,
Forth, to the laws of the ocean, we,
Builders on earth by laws of land,
Entrust this creature of our hand
Upon the calculated sea."

From *The Launch* by Alice Meynell,
1847–1922.

Prologue

By Christopher Nolan

'The Victorians allowed it. Then they did it. Then they turned their heads away and pretended it never happened.'

So runs a famous quote on the morality of the Victorians. A quotation that sums up much of the fascination of this book.

There have been other stories of this period, with fiction disguised as fact by romances of old diaries discovered in dusty attics. Although the manner in which these Journals came into my possession is a fascinating one, it has little relevance to the narrative. So I will let the words of Tom Goane speak for themselves.

My work as editor of these papers has been greatly aided by Tom Goane's own skill as a diarist. Although there are occasions when he relates incidents out of chronological order, and other—rare—times when he appears to write about scenes that he surely could not have witnessed personally, he always writes with great fluency and verve.

Since his schooling was not of the very best, I have sometimes altered his grammar and spelling. And in cases where his meaning seemed not entirely clear, I have taken the liberty of rephrasing the original. This will explain to the literary purists why there may be an occasional apparent word or phrase which seems to be more modern than Victorian.

The content of the Journals flows freely over a period of many years, and I have needed to do little to tidy them up. Where discretion called for it, I have on a small number of occasions taken the liberty of altering a name of a place, but virtually everything that you will read is in Tom Goane's own words.

There is an incident which appears a little later in this volume which deserves some passing comment. Generally speaking, Tom has been totally frank and honest, but in the passage relating to a lady he encounters while bird's-nesting in the grounds of a large house he becomes rather more coy. I will be more forthright. It is my opinion that the young lady is *not* the person that those suspicious minds might imagine. My own good taste forbids me to say more.

Where the original was perfectly comprehensible at the time in all matters, not every reader will be totally familiar with all aspects of Victorian life. Therefore, I have taken the precaution of inserting an infrequent footnote where I felt a passage needed some slight amplification.

My Publisher has asked me to make clear my relationship to the original writer of these Journals. I choose not to do so, out of respect for the memory of a dear friend. A lady who brought the papers to me and whose privacy and reputation I must continue to preserve.

This first volume of the papers covers most of Tom Goane's eventful childhood, and brings us up to the opening of the Great Exhibition on 1st May 1851.

Tom Goane was born on the 24th day of September in the year 1834. The day of the death of King Peter IV of Portugal. A day that began in London with an early autumn mist but brightened later. Weather that was, in some ways, to parallel the life of our hero.

But I have said enough. You will be waiting to read the adventures in his own words. I shall withdraw to the wings, making only one further comment to those of you who are intrigued and wish to know more of Tom Goane.

Later in this volume you will read how he encounters that madcap band of revolutionary artists who called themselves the PRB, the Pre-Raphaelite Brotherhood. Tom modelled, as did they all for one another, and can be seen clearly and identifiably on the extreme left of William Holman Hunt's painting *A Converted British Family Sheltering a Christian Missionary from the Persecution of the Druids.* Bare-chested and bare-footed, Tom Goane can be seen in the Ashmolean Museum at Oxford. It is unfortunate that the painting does not reveal his face.

And now I leave you in the hands of Tom Goane himself.

CHAPTER ONE

'Would you believe that Mister Charles Dickens, no less, used me as the model for that ruffian Fagin in his great work *Oliver Twist*? As true as I stand here.'

My oath! But if my Uncle Abraham had told that to one person, then he had told it to a full score. And it was not the most savoury titbit of conversation at the best of times. Or the worst of times.

And I might also allow that it was not even true. For I once had the pleasure of meeting Mister Dickens and asked him personally. Face to face. And he told me that the evil character of Fagin was actually founded upon a famous Hebrew fence named Ikey Solomons, who was tried for his crimes in 1830, just four years before my own birth.

But Uncle Abraham, resplendent in a dark suit and a towering hat, still told everyone who would listen that he was the true original. Aunt Eliza, a fur tippet hung rakishly around her wattled neck, ignored him, preferring to watch the astounding and unprecedented scenes about us.

A swell seated one along from us leaned over and hushed Uncle Abraham with a face as black as a sweep's elbow. 'Keep quiet, my good man, or I shall have you put out,' he said.

Now my Uncle Abraham was not the sort of a cove to be spoken to in that sort of manner. He smiled back at the swell, tipping his hat to the swell's lady, and said, as sweet as you please, 'The only putting out around here, cully, will be your teeth if you don't hold your noise.'

He had a ferocious smile did Uncle Abraham. I've even seen a brace of peelers step in the gutter when they saw that smile.

11

'Hush, Abe. There's his Reverence about to give us all a prayer.'

Aunt Eliza closed her eyes in what I think she imagined to be the right sort of expression of piety. It seemed to me that she was about to pray for more customers and cleaner girls. But then again, I knew my Aunt Eliza better than most, having been reared by her since my mother passed away.

And an odd sort of a rearing it was.*

While the good old Archbishop of Canterbury gave us his best speech and prayers, I looked around at the glittering throng that packed the great Crystal Palace. After a dull beginning to the day, the sun blessed us all with his presence, beating down through the miles of glass that made up the roof and walls of the place.

Although the tickets to get in cost three guineas for men and two for women, Uncle Abraham had managed to get us some marvellous seats. I'm told there were near twenty-five thousand souls crammed in there.

Sweating hot it was!

A fine lady in the row in front of us was mad when a sparrow left a visiting card on her silk dress. I heard that these birds had been a great worry during the early stages of the Exhibition, but the grand old Duke of Wellington, may he live for ever, solved the problem neatly. He told our Queen to 'Try hawks, Ma'am!'

They had, and they worked. But not entirely to everyone's satisfaction. Specially the woman in front of us.

Aunt Eliza had done nothing but fidget during the speech

* It will already be clear that Tom Goane wrote several parts of his Journals at a later date, which may account for an occasional apparent lapse of his memory. However, I have taken it upon myself to edit them into a sort of a chronological order. Since his description of the Great Exhibition is one of the earliest highspots in the diaries, I have used this to open this book. But I shall shortly allow Tom to recount, in his own words, his early history.

of Prince Albert. Not that I could blame the dear soul, as the Queen's husband is not the finest of speakers. Apart from a hideous thick accent, he delights in using a dozen words where one would be enough.

Looking back on that glorious day, I am delighted that I shared in the moment. And that I was privileged to have such an excellent seat. For that one must thank a benevolent Jehovah. For imagine how easy it would have been for luck to play us a sour trick.

When Uncle Abraham nicked that wallet, he had no way of knowing where it might leave us. But we were lucky, and could see everything perfectly. The light sort of broke up as it shimmered through the glass walls, making Her Majesty's pink dress look as though it had been spun from pearls beneath the sea.

Despite her face and figure, neither of which are the most favoured, I must admit that I admired her greatly that day.

But my mind wandered, and I only remember a little of the Archbishop's speech and prayers. He said that he was glad that there was no war or pestilence to blight our borders, making him sound like a dithering gardener. Anyway, it seemed foolish to me to say such a thing. Every man there was pleased we were not then at war. It was like saying that he was happy not to have a hatchet buried in his mitre, or whatever it is that they wear!

He went on, 'While we survey the works of art and industry all around us, let not our hearts be so lifted that we forget the Lord our God. As if our own power or the works of our own hands had gained for us this wealth. Riches and honour all come from God, who reigns over us all.'

Now I'm not sure that I agree with that either. It's all very well saying that God ought to take the credit. But I believe that you get what you get because of what you do to get it. I'll be the first to blame the Almighty when things start going amiss, but I'm not going to let him have the credit for things I earn by myself.

As soon as the Archbishop had finished this prayer, with Aunt Eliza sobbing heartily into her lace wipe, and Uncle Abe sizing up the back pocket of the gent standing in front of us, this choir gave out with a mighty bellow of singing. I don't mind a bit of a knees-up on a Saturday, and I love a visit to the Halls as much as the next man, but I can't say I take to this religious caterwauling.

While everyone was hallelujahing away fit to bust, I saw a very odd sight. All the nobs were pushing and shoving, ready to form up their procession around the Queen, when this yellow fellow elbowed his way forwards and threw himself flat on the red carpet, right in front of Vicky and her brood.

A real Chinaman, down to a long black pigtail. Like some of the greasy Lascar seamen that frequented Aunt Eliza's house. Turned-up toes on his clogs, and a sort of white shift. With a bright green silk robe over all. Little red cap like a smart Jew boy and a fan like one of the Cremorne whores. I'd never seen anything like it, and I reckon that neither had the party up there on the rostrum.

Heroic Albert takes one step forwards and two steps back, feeling for his sword, and damn near tripping over his own scabbard. Going all red at the wattles like a turkey that sees the chopper on its way. Half the ambassadors from St James all gasp at this, wondering if it's someone trying to do down the Royals.

Coolest there was the Queen. Like always. She looks down at the heathen who's still grovelling on the floor like he's dropped a florin. Says something to one of her aides, who moves on down, and helps up the Chinaman, and shows him to a place in the procession, just like he was the right-hand man of the Great Panjandorum.

Everyone was all hushed at this happening, and the whisper came back that he was indeed a man of note from the further countries of the East. But my Uncle Abe seemed transfixed with mirth, and leaned across to tell me that he knew the man and that he was far from what he pretended.

'Fly devil! Calls himself "Hee Sing" and he's bought an old junk and shows folk round it near Wapping at a bob a head. No more a real Chinee than me!'

I had seen the strangely rigged vessel on the Thames, and I was sure that my uncle was right. There was very little that went on in London that Abraham's berry-brown eyes missed. It sometimes seemed to me that Abraham was like a spider that sat at the centre of his web in the rookery off Castle Street, in Seven Dials. Feeling every movement of every strand. Ready to seek out that movement and make his own profit from it.

It may appear to you, reader, that I dislike my uncle and aunt. Because they sailed to the lee side of the law makes no difference to me. Tom Goane has sailed those waters himself for too long to think that the folk there are any different from the snobs in Chelsea or Camden.

No. I will always avow that I owe everything to those good-hearted people.

What if Aunt Eliza ran one or two houses where businessmen and senior clerks came to relax with ladies of spotless virtue? And what if her husband, Abraham Levy, sometimes took those things which weren't his by right? He never harmed a man by violence. Unless the said man did him harm first, of course. Nor did he plunder from those who could ill afford it.

He sometimes compared himself to the villain of the Greenwood, Robin Hood. Uncle Abraham certainly robbed mainly the rich. But the latter part of the ideal—about helping the poor—somehow passed him by. Nor do I think that Master Hood was such an unashamed Hebrew as Uncle Abe.

But now the official opening of the Great Exhibition was

nearly over, with Her Majesty sailing pinkly over the carpets with all her politicians and soldiers and courtiers in tow, like a little barge surrounded by an array of mighty leviathans. We had been told by a giant of an official at the main doors that we must all keep our places until the royal party had vanished on their own tour of exploration. Then, at a given signal, we would be free to tour ourselves.

This giant, in a red frogged coat with gold-laced buttons, checked our tickets with great care. Almost as though he felt that we were an unlikely threesome to have such an exalted position on this day of days. Had it not been for the great press around us I think that he might have stopped us to check our credentials.

I asked Uncle Abraham afterwards what steps he would have taken had this happened.

'Damned long ones, Tom,' was his reply.

'It says that it's a Greek Slave and that it's been carved by Hiram Powers. Funny name, Hiram. Doesn't sound English to me.'

'I think he's American, Uncle Abe.'

'I think it's nothing short of disgusting,' said Aunt Eliza, sniffing loudly. 'I just hope that it was covered up when the Queen passed by.'

'Passed out, more like. If she saw that,' sniggered my uncle.

I confess that I was interested in the statue. Purely on the grounds of art, you understand. Set against a background of brushed red plush, like you see on the swishest seats in the theatres, it was a large statue cunningly hewn from white marble. *The Greek Slave*, as Abe said. It dominated the section of the Exhibition given over to America, and there was a great crush around it.

It stood, one hand resting on a pedestal, hands darbied together with a double strand of chain. Quite unclothed. Her globes nicely rounded and one hand laid delicately over the fanny.

Personally I preferred the poses plastiques that Aunt Eliza put on for the gentry. But those women couldn't be confused with art. Not even on a foggy night in Wapping.

The Greek Slave wasn't the only bit of pulchritude on show in the Exhibition. There was a thing by a Belgian called *The Lion In Love*. This beast looking as drunk as a lord, with a naked strumpet on its back, gazing up at her while she cut his claws. Fair made me sick to see such sloppy nonsense, though Eliza was taken with it, falling to yet another fit of weeping at the beauty of it.

We spent much of the warm afternoon there, with only a short pause for some refreshment out in the Park, walking among the great throngs. I heard that there were nearly half a million there that day. Though that seems a number difficult to compass in the mind. There were boats out on the Serpentine, the air was filled with the blaring of band music, and the green trees competed with a host of brave flags, listing the nations that were there.

Although all the papers had been making much of the wonders to be seen, I was not overly impressed. Paxton's great building seemed to be more wondrous than most of the thousands of exhibits contained in it. It is difficult for me to convey to you the size and wonder of that Palace of Crystal, as Mister Punch called it. It glittered in the sunlight like a fairy castle, and it was the wonder of all eyes. I had been paying visits to Hyde Park for some weeks, charting its progress, but I had not been prepared for the sight of it, bustling with the colourful crowds, filled with trees and the wonders of our age.

Wonders that set me grinning behind my hand at their silliness. Not all of them. Don't think me some radical, intent only on mocking our country. There were many things, specially in the halls of engineering, that made my mind boggle.

But some of the other things . . .

I cannot imagine any occasion when I might want a knife with three hundred blades to it. Nor can I think of many times that a collapsible pianoforte would come in useful. And as for the walking stick that contained test-tubes *and* the apparatus for administering an enema!

Perhaps if three hundred costive men were cast away in a land that had a dozen concert-halls, each one separated from the others by difficult terrain.

As evening shaded towards night and the lights blazed out across the water, we paid a last tour of the Exhibition, Uncle Abraham declaring that he intended to get the fullest value for his eight-guineas-worth of tickets.

In we went, past the statue of King Richard the Lion-hearted and the monstrous twenty-ton lump of coal from the mines of the Duke of Devonshire. Eliza was feeling rather faint after the exertions of the day and insisted on a little further nourishment.

We managed to find our way through the still large crowds to the rooms set aside for the purpose of refreshment, although one could obtain free glasses of purified water throughout the Exhibition. Uncle Abraham was somewhat upset to find that there was a total ban on the sale of any intoxicating drinks, and subsided grumbling behind a foaming bumper of ginger-beer. I joined my aunt with a glass of lemonade, accompanied by four Bath buns and some potted meats.

All this placed a certain strain on me, and I was considering leaving quietly to find a spot behind some of the trees in the Park. When I recalled what I had read in the *Thunderer*. That a novel experiment was being tried for the first time at a large public gathering, by the introduction of public facilities.

By a whispered request of one of the attendants, now looking rather frayed at the edges after what must have been a hard day for him, I was directed to a discreet door at the rear of a mass of heavy foliage.

I returned from the cast-iron oasis feeling greatly relieved, only to find that Uncle Abraham and Aunt Eliza were involved in one of their frequent altercations, their voices creeping gradually up the scale, attracting the unwelcome attention of nearby visitors.

'I want to get back to the house, you old fumbler. You can stay here if you wish.'

'Eliza Levy! You call me a fumbler! A lousy dolly-mop like you with less furze on your bush than fleas on a scrubbed doorstep! Why if I were to ...'

Knowing only too well that these familiar discussions ended all too often in violence, and not wishing to be so involved, I heartily enjoined them to cease.

'Come now! The heat and walking have made you both tired. Why do you not both return to the ...' I was on the edge of saying 'rookery', which would have given away to the ring of listeners that we were not, after all, of the class that might expect to find itself in the Great Exhibition on that opening day.

Uncle Abraham looked up at me, with anger blazing in those red-rimmed pits of eyes. Eyes that would have once made me start back in fear. But that was years back. Now I topped him by several inches, standing a little over six feet, and having developed the muscles to carry it off.

'Why! If I were a few years younger, you thankless young blackguard!'

'If you were twenty years younger, Uncle Abe, I'd still be able to pick you up under one arm and carry you out of here. And with Aunt Eliza under the other arm, as well. Just think what would happen if any of the Law caught us bickering here and looked at those tickets you have in your waistcoat pocket. It would go hard for us all.'

The anger disappeared. Whatever else Abraham Levy might be, a fool he was not. Though he was prone to bitter rages, mostly directed against Eliza, they passed like the dew in the morning, and he was his normal even-tempered self again.

'Very well, young Tom. As usual, you speak more sense than your years. It *has* been a hard day, ain't it, Eliza?'

'Yes. It truly has. You've got your mother's sense, Tom Goane. If only the Good Lord hadn't seen fit in his infinite wisdom to take your ma away from us so sudden and in such a way . . .'

'Yes, Aunt. Now you and Abe bustle off home and pour out a warming noggin of gin and hot water. I'll have a last poke around here and be back directly.'

'Plenty of the quality this time o'nights laying around the worse for drink, Tom. You might cut a purse or two on the way.'

'More peelers around here than rats in Smithfield, you old fool. Now get along home with the both of you. The heat's addled both your heads.'

'For a boy of sixteen to speak to his lawful guardians so!' exclaimed Eliza Levy, gathering her skirts about her like a clipper facing a typhoon.

'Lawful, dearest Aunt?'

I knew that would hole her below the waterline, and it did. For she realised, as I had realised some years back in the middle '40s, that she and Abe had not a jot or a tittle of a real right to hold me to them.

Except that I was duly grateful to them, and if I had ever broken from them, then I would have been at risk to be taken in by the Parish, and perhaps 'prenticed to a sweep or sent packing down the mines. Or to spend my days in picking oakum or on the wheel. For I fear that an even temper has never been the strongest of my virtues, and a humble spirit is essential to survive in the workhouse.

'Why, you ungrateful and . . .'

'Now, now, dearest Eliza,' I said, seizing her round her ample waist and bussing her on both cheeks. 'Until the day I die I shall never forget my duty to both of you or the esteem in which I hold you both. Nor will you ever be far from my thoughts, wherever I may roam.'

It was a pretty little speech, and Aunt Eliza was much mollified by it, dabbing an errant tear from her eyes with a much-travelled wipe. On mutual good terms we parted, and I watched them walk away through the crowd, Uncle Abe's long, skinny arm across her shoulders, his head turning this way and that, ever on the look for either a chance of an easy penny or the blue uniform that haunted his nightmares.

And yet, I will say it once again to you. They were both wonderful people. Kind and generous to a poor orphan without a friend in the world.

The Pavilion of the Chinese people was surprisingly empty. Perhaps folk were turned against it by the news from the papers of the unhelpful attitude of the Chinese towards Prince Albert's great scheme. They had been given one of the largest areas in the whole exhibition and they had hardly sent enough to fill a church poor-box.

On the other hand, the industrious Swiss had been given one of the smallest pavilions and had been incensed to find that many of their offerings had been refused on grounds of inadequate space. Still, I imagine that you can have enough of yodelling, cheese and cuckoo clocks.

Many of the richest in the land had been canvassed by the Exhibition Committee to see if they had anything that could be used to fill up the Chinese area. They had responded magnificently, packing the Pavilion with rich carpets, statues and bits and pieces of china. Chinese china, that is.

If I could have been given ten minutes in there with a large sack, then Tom Goane need never have lifted his hand in labour again. I knew men in certain expensive shops who would have paid a fortune for some of that stuff and no questions asked. And I have an eye for the good stuff. A man can't live around Seven Dials for sixteen years without getting to know some odd skills.

I sat quiet on a bench, gathering my breath ready for the long walk back home, as I knew that it would be near impossible to pick up a hansom with those crowds around in the Park. When I heard someone sniffiing behind a huge hanging tapestry, ornamented with a vast flying dragon in scarlet and gold silk. Ever the gentleman where the weaker sex is concerned, I was up on my feet in an instant.

I pushed aside a suit of armour, looking for the source of the sound. As far as I could judge there was nobody else in that part of the Exhibition. Even the armour was without a chink.

But the Chinese Pavilion did have one noteworthy exhibit. And it was sitting on an over-stuffed seat, with its head buried in its hands.

Her hands.

Very pretty hands, to go with what seemed at first glance to be a rather pretty lady. Dressed in the sort of way that Aunt Eliza's girls liked to think they dressed but didn't.

A small bonnet set low on hair as black as a raven's wings. Her shawl looked good-quality lace. That was another thing that Seven Dials taught you. I would have looked to have obtained a good ten guineas even from the crookedest fence in Rotherhithe for that shawl and still left him a handsome profit.

A layered dress of green silk, each layer fringed with fine lace of a lighter green, with a broader edge at the bottom, brushing the floor as she sat sobbing to herself. The toe of one green satin shoe peeped out from under the skirt, with a buckle that my eye told me was much closer to gold than to pinchbeck.

A white parasol of French design lay ignored at her feet. And there was a glitter to its handle that dazzled the vision even in the failing light.

I coughed to attract her attention.

Had I placed a firecracker beneath her skirts I doubt that it would have startled her more than my sudden arrival. She leaped to her feet, dropping a dainty kerchief, both hands going to her mouth to stifle the gasp.

'Oh!'

'Madam, I make my most humble apologies for causing you to start in such a manner.'

You see that I can turn on the right sort of charm when the occasion calls for it. And my clothes were, though I say so as shouldn't, of the best.

'No. I...'

She was quite lost for words, and I took a step forwards to reassure her. Upon which she took three steps away from me, as though I was a beastly Frenchy—Monsieur Crapaud intent on ravishing her virtue.

Now seeing her face for the first time, I would not have blamed anyone for harbouring such thoughts. The lady was truly a stunner. Under that bonnet her face was shaped like a cupid's heart, framed with that marvellous hair, tugged back and fastened at the nape of her neck.

The shock had made her pale, but the colour sped back as she suddenly realised that she and I were alone together, half-hidden behind a vast Chinese tapestry and with evening rushing upon us. Tears hung like small pearls at the corners of her eyes. Damned pretty eyes! Brown, under delicate lashes. Dainty little nose, coming to a point. Sign of a determined nature, Aunt Eliza always said. And a proud chin, though my unexpected appearance had left it slightly a'tremble.

'I'm sorry if I . . .' As I spoke I took two more steps towards her, but the colour again fled from her cheeks and she retreated, near as a toucher sending a tray of fragile bowls spinning to the floor.

To ease the moment I stopped my advance and stooped to pick up her handkerchief, holding it out to her at the length of my arm. In the warm air of the Pavilion I couldn't help noticing the delicate scent that rose to my nostrils. She looked down at my hand as though I was offering her a viper. After all, it was only a wiper, if you will forgive my jest!

'You dropped this, I believe, Madam,' I said, making another damned elegant bow. Smart as one of Cardigan's cherry-bums.*

With a great effort the lady managed to recover something of her self-control, and reached out and took the kerchief from me, her gloved fingers, neat in natural kid, brushing mine.

'I . . . I am most gateful to you, and I apologise to you for my rudeness.'

'No apology is called for, madam,' says I. 'It is I who should be asking your pardon for startling you. Now, I shall withdraw, unless there is some other small service that I can render you?'

She hesitated, looking me up and down, and I could see that she was sizing me, trying to decide what sort of a fellow I was. Although I was still four months short of my seventeenth birthday, I was tall and well filled out. I grew my side-

* This is clearly a reference to the 11th Hussars of the infamous Lord Cardigan, who dressed his regiment from his own pocket, fitting them out in absurdly short jackets and extremely tight coloured trousers. They were to be butchered three years later under Cardigan's command as part of the Light Brigade charge at Balaclava.

whiskers to a good length, and pride myself that I looked more than presentable.

'You caught me, sir, at a moment when I was not myself. The heat in this place with its boring engines and endless samples have quite fatigued me and, to top all that, I have become separated from my escort and know not where he might be.'

'Then let me assist you to a place of egress.'

I confess that I was proud of that phrase. I recall one of my teachers beating the words 'entrance' and 'egress' into my head with as bony a set of knuckles as ever graced a human being.

'I would be most obliged to you, Sir.'

But she was still under the influence of the fit of vapours, from tiredness and the warmth, and as I offered her my arm she gave out a great sigh and swooned backwards, banging her head a sharp blow on the floor. Mercifully she dropped on one of the better carpeted sections, but she was, nonetheless, quite still, her senses fled.

I had often seen girls in a fearful state at the rookery, but all I knew from Aunt Eliza was that one had to loosen the clothing.

Beginning with the stays.

Most of the whores who swived away day and night for Aunt Eliza wore precious little. And few of them bothered with stays, except when they had a 'special' in, who liked something unusual in the way of garments. Or were in for a dose of discipline and fustigation.

And none of them was covered so thick with clothes as this young lady. There was layer upon layer, thicker than blowflies on a pile of horse manure. Though that is an indelicate way of putting it for such a pretty person.

I had scarcely set my hand burrowing up under the layers of silk and cotton of the dress and the interminable petticoats before the lady began to recover. It was not my wish to be caught with my fingers up her skirt, so I made haste to withdraw them.

Above the stockings, they had encountered what felt like plush drawers, marking her as a true woman of quality, and I was somewhat disappointed that my exploration was to be so short-lived.

But it was not.

I was wearing a new pair of gold and onyx cuffs to my shirt that Abe had given me in honour of the occasion. He was specially pleased that they had a monogram that was my initials. Well, truth to tell, they were not *quite* my initials. They were actually a 'T' and then an 'L' and then what looked like a hooked 'K'. But at least there was the 'T' there, clear to see. And when one obtained cuffs in the manner of Uncle Abraham, it was too much to expect that all the initials would be correct.

But it was these cuffs that were my downfall.

In some way they become caught around a piece of lace hanging loose from the bottom of the lady's drawers, holding my hand quite fast between her legs.

A pleasant enough predicament at most times, and one that Tom Goane counted among his greatest pleasures. But this was no thrupenny bung-up.

I was kneeling over her, my left hand leaning in the thick pile of the carpet, my face only inches from hers, when her eyes opened.

Blinked.

Fluttered like a dove's wings.

Closed again.

Opened.

Her mouth half opened in a vague smile, and I vow that I felt her wriggle her legs against my hand. Just at that moment, a bell rang somewhere in the body of the main hall of the Exhibition, and she opened her eyes wider.

'Oh sir! What are . . . ?'

I smiled in an attempt to reassure her that my intentions were as honourable as might be expected. But my tongue has a sad habit, at times of great emotion, of becoming tangled up with my mind, so that the words that leave my brain never reach my mouth in the same order.

'I wished only to open your clothing and raise your legs.'

That was what I intended to say.

'I wished only to raise your clothing and open your legs.'

That was what I actually said. As much to my horror as to hers.

'Really!' But it seemed to me that she was more amused than shocked, and I took new heart. I had more than half anticipated that she would slap my face and call for the attendants. Which would have left me with the unchivalrous duty of striking her unconscious and taking to my heels.

'Yes. I mean, no. But I have become entangled with your underpinnings. Perhaps I might . . . ?'

'Yes. Perhaps you might, though this is damnably presumptuous when we have not yet been introduced.'

'I'm sorry.' I tried to rise, quite forgetting that my hand was still half a yard up her skirt, and succeeded only in tumbling half a'top of her, my left hand accidentally landing on her swelling bubbies.

Where I stabbed my finger on the pin of a brooch of amethysts and opals that held the bodice together.

'Ouch!'

'Poor boy. What's wrong now?'

She made no attempt to remove my hand or to try and free her legs.

'I fear that you have pricked my finger.'

That was what I intended to say.

My sense of delicacy forbids me to mention the words that I heard my tongue utter, though I suspect that the more frank-minded among you might make a shrewd guess.

And it was at this moment, overhearing my words, that her escort finally found her.

And me.

He was tall. Very tall indeed. Approaching six feet three or four inches. Wearing a black cloak, which swirled open to reveal a crimson lining. And a silver-knobbed cane of black malacca. His face was partly in shadow, but he sported a heavy moustache.

'Am I interrupting something, Christabel? Should I withdraw now and return and skewer this young puppy after you have concluded your business?'

'No,' I said.

'Oh,' she said.

'Let me explain,' I said.

'Let me,' she interrupted.

'I am utterly disinterested in anything you might have to say, my bravo,' he said.

'But . . .' I said.

'Jonny . . .' she said.

'Christabel,' he said, 'either you rise now or I shall run the grave risk of spitting you as well as him.'

And he twisted the handle of the cane with his dark gloves, withdrawing a few inches of gleaming steel. My cry checked him from sliding the remainder of the swordstick into view.

'You must let the lady explain, sir.'

'I must, must I? Very well, Christabel, I will allow you precisely one minute to narrate these amazing events, and then I will kill the child.'

With a rending noise I finally contrived to free my right hand and I rose quickly to my feet, reaching down to help the lady, but she chose to remain on the carpet. The toff took a cautious step away when he saw that I came close to matching him in height and wasn't the child he'd imagined.

The blade flickered again in his hand, and I noticed that he wore a heavy gold ring on the index finger of his right hand, with an odd design. What looked at a glance like a horse's head.

'My oath! You're a big fellow! Come, Christabel, the gallant fellow would aid you to your feet. Take his hand, will you?'

Her voice shaking with tension, the lady looked at the man, pulling herself up with the aid of my hand in a flurry of lace. 'Really, Count! Your jealousies are becoming tedious to me.'

Sheathing the sword yet again, the stranger clapped his hands in sardonic applause. 'My dear Christabel! You are too good. You could act Helena Faucit herself off the stage. I lose you in the crush, and when I track you down in this quiet and dark corner, I find you flat on your back with this puppy groping your tits with one hand and rogering you with the other, while using language that I would not wish to hear in the presence of a lady.'

'Sir! You insult the lady, and . . .'

'Hold your tongue, whelp. Well, Christabel! I am waiting for your explanation.'

Her brown eyes flashing angrily, the lady stepped closer to him, where he stood still, his face masked in the spreading pool of shadow. Her bosom heaved and she stamped her dainty foot in a rage.

'If you will not listen to the truth, then it is all up between us. I was overcome with the heat and tired and vexed beyond endurance at losing you. Aye, I was saddened, for I thought that I might not see you again on this great day. And here, in this . . . "quiet and dark corner" as you call it, I fainted away. Alone and in deepest misery.'

And she began to cry quietly, letting her hands droop at her sides, making no attempt to check the flow of tears that ran clear down her nose, pattering on the floor. Her escort—

had she called him 'Count'? — clenched his fists, throwing his stick on the seat, where I watched it with some relief.

Finally he reached out and grasped her to him, squeezing her in a hug like a bear, and I saw that his shoulders too were shaking with mighty sobs.

'My dearest sweet one. Please stop weeping. Of course I believe you.'

'And this gallant young man came to my rescue, and was doing his best to restore me when you appeared.'

'I regret only that I lacked any sal-volatile. I did not expect to need it here.'

I was trying to lighten the atmosphere with a jest, but they both took my comment seriously and nodded at me. The Count gently set his lady aside and looked at me. 'We're both in your debt, young man.'

It was now possible to see him more clearly, and a fine and imposing figure he cut. Eyes that looked as black as jet in the gloom of the Chinese Pavilion, with brows that hung over them like a mummer's false hair. White teeth which gleamed as he smiled at me. Although I was sure that I'd never met him before, there was something familiar about him. Nothing that I could quite bring to the front of my mind, and yet he made me feel somewhat uneasy.

'I was endeavouring to loosen the lady's garments as my Aunt Eliza had told me when I unluckily caught . . .'

'Eliza? Did you say that the name of your aunt is Eliza? Eh?'

'Yes, sir, I did.'

He looked as though he was about to question me further but checked himself, turning away from me with a half-laugh that puzzled me, for it seemed to token something that I could not understand.

'Well, enough, my boy. The lady is restored and there's an end to it, and I trust that you'll behave like the gentleman

I take you for and shake my hand to seal our new understanding of each other.'

'Why, with all my heart do I,' I replied, taking his gloved hand in my bare palm, wincing at his power, and putting all my efforts into showing I was no milksop, and squeezing him back, giving as good as I got. So we stood locked together for a moment, and then he laughed again and turned to the lady, who had been watching the test of strength with a secret smile at us.

'Now. Now we are friends, we must know who we are. Sir, pray allow me to introduce my companion, Miss Christabel Meadows.'

I bowed low, taking her hand in mine and pressing my lips to it.

'And I, my heroic young blade, am called Count Jonathan Yglesias.'

I saw that he was watching my face closely for any sign of recognition.

'You are . . . !'

He wasn't disappointed.

'I repeat that I am Count Jonathan Yglesias. And you, I think, are . . . ?'

'My name is Goane. Thomas Goane.'

The girl looked at me in amazement, her jaw dropping to her ample chest. 'Jonny! He's Tom Goane! Blind me and . . . ! What an oddity.'

Yglesias saw the bewilderment on my face and smiled. 'Perhaps we should now leave this Great Exhibition and take my carriage. We can talk over a bite of dinner. I think that we will all three have much to talk about.'

He was right.

CHAPTER TWO

EDITOR'S NOTE: *I am sure you are all wondering who this mysterious Count Yglesias is, and who is his attractive companion? This Christabel Meadows, who met our narrator in such informal surroundings? What do they know of each other, and why is Tom Goane so amazed to learn the man's name?*

These questions are all perfectly natural, and all will be answered in the fullness of time. But, as I have said earlier, to aid the dramatic narrative I have taken the liberty of using my editorial licence and placing this sequence of the opening of the Great Exhibition in Hyde Park in 1851 at the beginning of the book.

We will now resume Tom Goane's Journals at their very beginning. Chronologically this takes us back to the time when he was three, and a young girl of eighteen was taken from her bed to be told that she was no longer Princess Alexandrina Victoria.

She was the Queen of the greatest Empire on Earth.

We will travel back in time to that day: 20th June 1837.

I remember a huge man with wild hair and a hooked nose tossing me up in the air and shouting out, 'The King is dead! We have a Queen, Tom. A fine young Queen!'

I realised later that this, my earliest memory, must have been my Uncle Abraham, intoxicated on cheap gin, celebrating the change of monarch in 1837. Old King Billy—William IV—had finally lost his grip on this earthly life and had shuffled away upstairs to join his ancestors.

And he had left the throne of England to young Victoria. It meant the end of the British ties with Hanover, but this, of course, I only knew years later. When I understood about how the Salic Law operating there meant a girl couldn't inherit. I recall that the eldest son of the Duke of Cumberland took over the Hanoverian throne.

But what of me? Who was I? Where was I? What was I?

I was an orphan. The other children that scampered barefoot about the rookery told me that. Not mockingly, for half of them had no father to speak of, and the rest no mother either.

My memories of those early days are scattered and very confused. It is only now, that I come to begin these Diaries, that I see what mysterious events really must have been. When I was a child, I saw as a child.

Those monsters with their shining golden buttons and their towering hats of gleaming black. Who ruffled my hair and laughed in deep voices. And who held magic wands that made harsh, scaring noises that frightened me and made me run and hide my snotty nose in Aunt Eliza's skirts.

They were peelers with their rattles, which they used for years until they found whistles of more value.

And the rookery off Castle Street saw plenty of visits from peelers. Never alone. Often in gangs of four or five. Seven Dials wasn't a good place to be on your own, if you didn't belong there or have business there.

When the nobs came along to goggle at us, they brought keepers. Corinthians, some of them as black as a peeler's hat. Who guarded them from the robbers and cut-purses who thronged there as busy and secretive as the rats. Maybe even less bold.

I recall, and I can only have been about five, being attacked by a brace of rats. Huge lean beasts, brindled, with long yellow teeth. They had tried to take a crust of bread from my hand, and I resented it. One nipped me on the hand, before I picked it up in my chubby little fingers . . . and bit its head clean off its body.

33

Uncle Abraham was very proud of me for that, and I believe there were ructions between him and Eliza about it. He wanted to exhibit my talent for rat-killing to the gentry at a crown a head, but she stopped him.

I was lucky to have them as guardians, for they were among the aristocrats of the underworld of London. And it never occurred to me that there was anything wrong with the manner in which they earned their tin. For most of their friends were also folk who lived on the further borders of honesty.

Yet none harmed me.

Uncle Abraham was sometimes hard on me when he was in drink, which was more frequent in those early days of my life. But Aunt Eliza was there to protect me, and rub goose grease on my cuts and bruises. Except when affairs in her house of Mithras took her attention from me. Either a gentleman wouldn't pay his way. Or one of the girls was causing trouble.

I have since read that one house in fifteen in all London was a pegging crib like Eliza's. It seemed far more than that to me.

The early years passed in a blur of lively action. There was always something on. Someone to talk to. Someone to play with.

I was blissfully ignorant of what was happening in the world outside Seven Dials. It was a world that was bounded for me by Broad Street to the north and by Long Acre to the south. By Drury Lane to the east and by Crown Street to the west.*

I know we fought the Pathans on the North-West Frontier when I was only about four, as the house was filled with grim men in uniform. When I was five there was a deal of joking about what the girls in the house called the 'Queen's

* The border of this area to the west now would be Charing Cross Road, which wasn't opened until 1887.

Crib Debate'. I laughed with the others at it, but I didn't comprehend it then. Nor do I now, though I know there was some problem of Whig ladies serving the Queen and it became an issue and Sir Robert Peel was unable to form a government on it.

These were the years of the Chartist riots, but little of this was seen in London, and nothing of it within the labyrinthine houses and warrens of Seven Dials. Just as the troubles of outside rarely penetrated the walls and tunnels, so there was little rejoicing there when Victoria married that German muzpot, Albert.

Prime Ministers came and went as regular as clockwork dolls. Peel and Melbourne. Melbourne and Peel. And not a scrap of difference between them that we could see.

I recall Uncle Abraham being excited when a new paper was formed in London. I would have been about seven, and he insisted on quiet in our rooms while he read it through. But like most things with Uncle Abe, he became irritated at having to pay good money for it, and so the *Jewish Chronicle* no longer appeared in our house.

It must have been round about the time that I was seven or eight when I came to realise that I wasn't quite as other children around. For most of them at least had some idea of who their mothers had been, if not their fathers as well. I had simply assumed that I had somehow been 'found', or taken from the workhouse as a baby.

For no reason that I can now remember, I asked Aunt Eliza about what had happened to my mother. She had been cutting up some meat for a stew, and singing to herself. After my question it all went still, like a forest as a man passes through.

'Your mother?' she said, trying to buy time for herself.

'Yes, Auntie. Who was my mother? And,' as an afterthought, 'my father?'

My aunt laid down the knife and wiped her hands down

the front of her dress. To this day I can see the bloodstains on the printed cotton.

'Sit down, Tom, and I'll tell you all I know. Your Uncle Abraham and I have agreed that when we thought you were old enough to be told. Then we'd tell you. It ain't we didn't want to, you understand. We wasn't trying to keep it a secret from you.'

I sat down by the small fire that smoked away in the corner of the room, with some of the greasy tendrils making their way up the narrow chimney, and more of them winding around the low ceiling and staining the walls.

It was an odd tale.

I was amazed to learn that my mother had been the niece of Eliza. Named Christine Florence Harvey. A woman of quite angelic beauty according to Eliza, and at that age I believed her every word, imagining my departed mother as a pale-skinned lady with bright yellow hair and a golden ring around her head.

Although Aunt Eliza hemmed and hawed her way around the matter, I gathered her drift. That perhaps she had not been married when I was on the way.

'There was this sailor, you see, Tom. A fine strapping fellow he was. On one of His Majesty's ships of the line. On the way to being an orficer, I wouldn't wonder. He would have married your ma, if he'd got to know of it. But he was killed fighting the French. A cannonball cut him in half when he was capturing this Froggy ship all on his ownsome.'

I confess that this picture also stayed with me for some time. Until I became schooled, in fact. When I discovered that we hadn't been fighting the French at the time. A small but significant point.

And the tale of the cannonball was blurred a week or so later when I ventured to inquire of my uncle about my late father.

'Who?' was his response.

'My father.'

'What's that old cat been telling you, my dearest child? Nothing foolish about mysterious nobs, I hope.'

I couldn't imagine what he meant by that.

Nor for many years later.

'The seaman.'

His face cleared like an alley in a thunderstorm. 'Oh, the sailor!'

'What of him, Uncle Abraham?'

He wrinkled his forehead with the effort of trying to think. Do keep in mind the fact that Abe was rarely less than half-drunk, and often at least four times that.

'He was a brave sailor and he's dead?'

It was more of a question than an answer.

'Yes.'

'Drownded, he was. Drownded dead as mutton. Never found his body.'

'Not cut in half by a cannonball?'

'Did she say that?'

'Yes, Uncle.'

'Damn her! Well, now I recall it, there was some tale of a ball that hit him. Cut him clean in half.' Triumphantly. 'And *then* he was drownded and no trace of his corpse.'

So there was an oddity to begin with.

But there was more.

'Your mother was a marvellous woman, Tom Goane, and don't you forget it. But she was ruined. Brought low by bad company, and I could tell more than that if I'd a mind to it.'

Even when helpless with drink, neither Abe nor Eliza ever let on that there was more of a mystery about me and my birth. But there was my name. If my mother's name was Harvey, and Abe's name was Levy, then where did Goane come from?

It was by a lucky stroke of chance that I found out.

37

It was a fine sunny day. Very hot, as it had been for many days. Cool at night with a mist off the river. The best sort of weather for old King Cholera to rule. They dropped like flies, and there were enough flies about to begin with.

Eliza had sent me off on an errand for her, but I'd scarcely crossed the road when I found I'd clean forgot where she'd said I was to go. Was it to One-Eyed Nell or to Scabby Anne? I went back intending to ask, and crept up the stairs, as I usually did, in case we had visitors.

My aunt had a friend with her, and they were both knocking back the hot water and gin as if they had been given special news from heaven that tomorrow had been cancelled.

The stairs up to my room creaked like the Devil, but I contrived to sneak up them, past the open door of what Aunt Eliza liked to call her withdrawing-room. There, by sitting as quiet and huddled as a country vicar, I was able to spy between the banisters and hear what they were saying.

There was an air of gloom to their talk. Her friend was Gimpy Jenny, a mulatto girl who worked in a house two doors down from ours. Although she had been crippled when a carriage turned over on her as a child in the Indies, she still managed to attract a large clientele for her services.

'I've never regretted 'avin' all me teeth drawn in that fang-chovey in Lisle Street, Eliza,' she was saying. 'Helped me to keep me health in all this sickness. You 'ear that Cheatin' Tony was took yesterday?'

'Yes, I did hear something of it. Cholera, wasn't it?'

The sound of glass tinkling against glass, and liquid gurgling.

'Yes. Bloody flux and all. They're buryin' 'im on the morrow. Rotten dog he was, that Tony. Steal pennies from his mother's eyes. I'll drink to 'im now 'e's gone.'

There was a silence, broken only by the noises of drinking and a large belch from one of them.

'Manners!'

From Gimpy Jenny.

'Not like when a loved one gets took, Eliza.'

'No. I'll never forget the way the Good Lord took the mother of that little waif, Tom. This sort of weather it was. It'd rained for days, back in '34. Then all the gutters choked up with rubbish and that. Out comes the sun and out comes the flies. And they started going down all over the town. Christine, that was his mother, was never well after his delivery. Awful confinement it was. She was in labour for three days and four nights. I was with her.'

Much tut-tutting from the other woman. I was getting cramps in my knees and I stretched to find a more comfortable position.

'Then she has him. Fine healthy boy he was. And is, thank God. But she was never well, and it was no surprise to Abe and me when the fever took her off a few days later. Have another glass, Jenny.'

'Don't mind if I do.'

It was sweltering hot up on those narrow stairs, twisting and twining to the top of the old building. As I leaned back and peered up into the gloom, it seemed like a chimney vanishing up there. Only the day before one of my playmates had died, trapped in a chimney.

He was seven. Apprenticed to a sweep a month earlier. Trouble was, he had too much flesh on his bones. Powerful hard it was, for those that went sweeping. I saw little Joey each night, after he'd ended training, and he was always weeping with the pain.

Climbing boys need hard skin on knees and elbows to wriggle their way up, and Joey was only a scrap of a kid. So his master made him stand for hours every day right by a roaring fire while he scraped away at his arms and legs with brushes soaked in a solution of brine strong enough to bring out your fingernails. So his elbows and knees bled and hardened with the salt.

Went on every day for two weeks. The rubbing and the bleeding and the fire and the brine.

I tell you, with my hand on my heart, that I was never so glad for my good fortune in getting schooling as when I ever thought of Joey.

Miserable end, fit for not even a mad dog.

Joey was scrambling up one of the parlour chimneys of a fine gent's house off Pall Mall when he got caught in a fork. Biggest danger for a climber was his belt. You see these chimneys are so narrow and tight, and choked with thick soot and ash, that a lad has to climb with one arm up over his head and the other down by his thighs. And push and wriggle and pull. But you had to wear a stout belt, otherwise if your trousers came off you were trapped by them.

Seems that Joey's belt turned over with the pushing, sort of folding double at the front, and he couldn't get a hand to it.

And so he died.

But I was writing about my aunt and her talking of my late mother.

The gin was still flowing, and her tongue was getting looser, almost as if she was being forced to talk. To tell someone.

'Of course, and this only between you and me and the gatepost, but I have my thoughts on who his real pa is, you know.'

'My lips is sealed tight as a Jew's wallet. Ooh, sorry Eliza. I forgot there for a moment about you bein' wed to one of them. But go on.'

'Well,' and here my aunt dropped her voice to a low sort of whisper, making it hard for me to hear. But by straining my ears I was able to make most of it out.

'You know that I've mentioned once or twice the way we gets a bit of tin, now and again, you understand, and it

40

always comes the same way. Anymously . . . Amoninously
. . . Amninom . . . Bugger it! We don't know who sends it.
And it's made clear that it's for Tom. And there's been a
note telling us to keep him from harm, and not to 'prentice
him. No matter what. It's my belief that he's to be schooled.'

'Ooh. Wouldn't that be somethin'?'

I was near as shocked as Gimpy Jenny. The idea that I
might be educated had never entered my head. It was just
something that brats like me never did. And these suspicions
of a benefactor! I listened even harder.

'Well, that's to come, and we must be patient. But as for
what passed . . . It all started a few days after my poor dear
niece went before to join that celestial band a'plucking their
harps in everlasting love.'

Aunt Eliza was a great scanner of religious pamphlets,
notwithstanding having married a Hebrew.

'I was sitting here, in that very chair where you are now,
and it was near evening. Abe was out on . . . business. The
mite was a'laying in his cradle, sucking on his finger-ends.
When I hears a foot on the stairs.'

If she didn't get a move on, then there was going to be an
accident on the stairs right now. I'd been guzzling water
from the pump in the back court, trying to keep cool, and it
was having its effect.

'The room's as dark as anything, with just the one lamp.
Stood on that table at your elbow, Jenny. And I looks up,
thinking it's a gentleman who's come for service and used
the wrong door by mistake. You know. But there's a knock
on the door. Quiet. Like a scratching noise. I gets up ready
to open it, when it opens on its own, and there stands this
huge man. Very tall he was, all shrouded in a black cloak.
Pulled up over his head in a hood, like a monk.'

'Oooh! I'd probably have pissed myself at it. I'd 'ave
thought it were a ghost.'

'No ghost. Big man. Made the boards creak, I recall.

41

Couldn't see nothing of his face, hidden in the dark as it was. But his voice was soft as rubbing your finger over velvet. And deep. Lovely voice. Asks me if I'm Mrs Levy, and if I'm caring for a babe.'

I was becoming more and more interested in the story.

'I wonders if he's after me as a baby-farmer, come to take it away, and I'm about to say nothing. When little Tom gives out a cry, and he looks round. "That the child of Christine Florence Harvey?" he says. I asks him what's it to him, and he comes closer and grips my face between his gloved fingers. As I live and breathe, Jenny, I thought he was about to pull my jaw away from my face. I could feel my teeth a'creaking in my gums. "Lie to me, woman, and you will regret it for the last few miserable days of your life." So I tells him the truth.'

'I knows just what you means about teeth creakin'. Did I say that I was glad I'd had mine out? Makes some of the gentry pleased, and all. I makes a middlin' livin', just out of not 'avin' me teeth.'

Eliza was cross at being interrupted. 'Yes. If I've heard of your bleedin' teeth once, Jenny, then I've heard tell a hundred times.'

'Sorry, Eliza. Go on.'

Mollified, my aunt carried on with her enthralling tale of the past. 'He walks slowly over, hood still tugged down over his face, and stands there, quiet, looking down at the babe in its cot. I'm about to speak up, and ask him what the hell he's wanting, when he turns to me. "That child will not want while I live," he says. "There will be money. Not too much to tempt you, but enough to aid a good education for him. It is a boy?" I tells him that it is. Then he puts down a sovereign and warns me what'll happen if either me or Abe tries to make off with it.'

The house is quiet, though I can hear the death-cart making a call a few yards down the road there. A woman screaming and carrying on as her man or her child is wheeled away to the pits. We heard that sort of thing every summer.

'Go on, dearie,' says Gimpy Jenny.

'Well, as true as I sit here . . . more gin? There. As true as I sit here, he was a real gent. I sees lots of them, and I can tell. This was a toff.'

'He just left the money and went?'

'No. Though I do think as how that was his intent. He puts down the money, and looks down at the babe again. Asks his name again, and I tells him. Without another word, he's off to the door. And I hears what sounds like Abe in the street outside, calling to someone.'

I had the trembly feel that my world was about to be altered for ever, and I hugged my knees to stop them shaking.

'I wasn't going to let it pass without a question. You see, it seemed to me that this must be the gent that poor Christine had been with. Maybe the father of Tom, and I wanted to give the child a name other than Levy. So I calls out and asks him his name just as he rushed out on the stairs.'

'What did 'e say? Did 'e say 'is name was Goane, then? Did 'e?'

Aunt Eliza dropped her voice even lower. 'Yes. Just as he was goin'. He turned and called out. "Can't stop. I'm Goane." Those were his words. "I'm Goane." So there.'

So there.

CHAPTER THREE

Uncle Abraham once, and only once, made the cardinal error of appropriating the money set aside by my mysterious benefactor for my schooling.

It was not a mistake that he made more than once.

A six-inch nail hammered through the knee-cap can be more efficacious than all the words in the world. And the mere threat of that nailing can be enough. Certainly the threat was enough as far as Uncle Abe was concerned.

I suppose it happened when I had been at my private school for about two years. Which would make me near enough to ten. I recall it would be 1844, as there was much outcry in the rookeries about the new Factory Act that the softies had just introduced. It limited the hours that a child of eight could work to a mere six and a half per day. They would crush all initiative and hope with their repressions.

Shortly after I overheard the conversation between my Aunt Eliza and Gimpy Jenny, I stopped my habitual activity of playing around the alleys and courts of the district, and began my education. Most dame schools in those days were paid for at the rate of about sixpence per week. Mine cost a shilling.

Those days passed like smoke in a wind. I recall that I hated the succession of lean, hungry-faced men who battered knowledge into me. And yet I now see that I owe them a debt of a sort. Without them I would be nothing. And know nothing.

But they were miserable times, and I will not speak of them now. There was an attempt when I reached the age of ten to get me into a public school. It failed.

And all this paid for by the mysterious man in the cloak.

I finally admitted to Aunt Eliza that I had heard what she said to Gimpy Jenny, and she was greatly put out by it. But I assured her that I could be relied upon to hold my tongue, and she and Abe consulted on it, and it was agreed that none of us should ever speak of it again.

Uncle Abraham was angered by the news that his wife had blabbed to another whore, and promised us trouble if the gentleman came to learn of it.

Oddly enough, the danger of Jenny telling what she had learned vanished only a day or so after that family meeting. And in a most peculiar fashion.

Jenny had been a middling sort of a harlot, with clients who came from high and low. On this day, she was pulling a toff down by the warehouses over Shadwell way. Far out of her usual beat.

It seems that she was doing him a turn out in the open, when a large object fell on her head. The man, who the only witness said was a tallish fellow in a cloak, scarpered in time. The large object, which was a pianoforte, fell in a mysterious way from an upper floor of the warehouse, crushing poor Jenny to the floor.

'Sad really,' said Aunt Eliza. 'Jenny was always fond of music.'

My belief is that it was someone with a grudge against the gent who was her customer, and Jenny got herself killed by mistake. Of course, there are other possible interpretations of what transpired, but that is the one that I personally find most likely.

One of my greatest wishes at that time was to try to track down my benefactor. Perhaps I was really of noble — or even royal — blood! The idea entranced me, and several times I came close to being collared by the peelers as I went around aiding Uncle Abraham in maintaining the family's fortunes.

For the money for my education was spent on that. And I was a growing fellow who ate well and drank more than a little. Yet brought nothing in.

So when Uncle Abe went off on some job or other, then Tom Goane was at his elbow.

I mentioned the time that my education money was misused by my uncle. Perhaps I should tell you something more of it.

Two years in the private school there had brought me the ability to read and to write a fair hand, though I always found, and still do find, that numbering and calculating is far from easy. I fear that I descended from the mathematical carriage when it passed the stops marked 'Algebra Halt' and 'Trigonometry Junction'.

Like many another boy I ended my schooling with small Latin and less Greek, though it was damnably uncommon for any urchin around Seven Dials to have an idea of either. Not that I didn't envy them their freedom. There were times when I would have changed places with the smokiest climber on a hot summer's afternoon when a steel rule across my fingers drummed home those absurd words 'Hic, haec, hoc', and their idiotic brothers 'Huius, huius, huius.'

My belief, for what it is worth, is that those things are a foolish joke put about by bored pedagogues. Surely the greatest Empire in the world, before our own that is, would not have stood in the Capitol and babbled such ninny-hammered stuff and nonsense at one another.

It was a specially hot afternoon that Uncle Abe and Aunt Eliza had one of the worst ding-dongs that I recall. A Monday, and I was to take in my weekly shilling, but it was not there. Aunt Eliza sent me from their presence, but I heard it all from my small room at the top of the house. From my dormer window I could clamber out on the tiles and just catch a glimpse of the golden dome of St Paul's Cathedral, and I sat there, hearing them going at it way below.

There was the sound of crying, and I was sure I heard blows. The front door slammed shut, and I peered over the guttering and saw Uncle Abraham, monstrously shorter from that height, stamp off towards the corner of the road, turning in the centre of the street to shake his fist at the house and bellow a curse.

When I went back down, I found Aunt Eliza tying up her cape with fingers that shook. Her eyes were red with crying, and I saw a purple bruise swelling near her right cheek. A fine thread of dark blood inched from her nostrils, and her lips were swollen.

She hardly saw me as I came in, and continued muttering to herself in an angry whisper that quite frightened me, as I had seen them have many a set-to but never with her like that.

'I'll learn him,' she said. 'See if I don't. Taking your tin, and him not having real need of it. Just trying to show what a mighty man he is. Well, we'll see. See if *he* thinks he's such a mighty man.'

I realised that she was talking about two different men when she said '*he*' and 'he'.

'What's happened?' I asked.

'Never mind.'

'Tell me, Aunt. I beg you. I've never seen you taking on so.'

She turned and looked at me. 'I'm goin' out, Tom. And I may be a little time. I have to try and find someone who doesn't take to being found. But I know of a way of getting a message, though it was only to be used in times of peril or hardship. So I shall be back later. Take care and don't get into no mischief, there's a good lad.'

I could tell she was greatly moved as she kissed me on the cheek. A thing she never did.

As to where she went, and who she saw, I can only hazard a guess.

But she came back when the lamps were being lit out west and the first girls were coming to the house for the night. And she was laughing. Giggling, maybe. Like she'd had too much to drink but had enjoyed it.

I came and sat down with her in the withdrawing-room, and once again she scarcely noticed me. She said one thing that stuck in my mind.

'All dark,' she said, 'but I saw his ring gleaming. Just like a dragon's head it was.'

'What was?'

'Just like a dragon's head. Eh? Never you mind, Tom, and keep your lips buttoned close. Do you hear?'

'Yes, but . . .'

'No buts, young man. Tomorrow you'll be to your schooling again, and no worries. I doubt that you'll miss a day again. Not now. But keep your mouth close.'

That night, Uncle Abraham didn't come home. He was often late when he was out on work, but this was different. Aunt Eliza expected him to return. Hours drifted by, and the men came and went in the house. The charvering part of the house, that is. I slept well. Always did. Hope I always will. But I woke in time to hear the bells ringing the hour. I could see out across the roof-tops, and it was near light. That would have made it near five, that time of the year.

It somehow felt as though something was amiss, and I quickly put on a thin robe and crept down. I heard someone talking in their bedroom—Abe and Eliza's—and I thought he must have taken a close call from the Law and had to scarper quick into hiding.

Yet, there was only one voice. That of my aunt. Talking quietly to herself. I made my way to the door of the room which stood a little ajar.

Through the golden crack I could make out Aunt Eliza, wearing only a cotton shift, brushing her hair by the single light of a brass lamp, set on the table at the head of their big mahogany bed.

After I had stayed a few moments, I moved away, and crept once again up the stairs, past the corner where one of the girls had told me the bogeyman lived, and into my own room, where I lay awake until breakfast, puzzled by what I had heard.

Aunt Eliza's religion bordered, frankly, on the sanctimonious, and I had never heard her at prayers before. But below me, she was still pattering out a plea to the Deity.

'I didn't mean him to be hurt bad,' she said. 'I know he's only a crooked old Jew, Jesus, but please let him be brought home safe and well. My life without Abe . . . Abraham . . . would be an empty vessel, Jesus. Please let him be all right. And let what I done not be the cause of it. Despite what I was told by . . .'

And at that tantalising point her voice faded away into a meaningless mumble.

It was nearly noon on the following day, and I had returned for a new slate pencil, when I witnessed the return of the wandering Abraham. And a sorry spectacle he made. The urchins tailed him, making much play with fingers to their noses and farting noises with their mouths to show what manner of a mess he was.

Someone, or knowing his temper several men, had taken him and thrown him in a midden. Not just thrown him in, but taken staves and pushed him under. And given him a sound drubbing on top of all.

That night the house was very quiet, and I was doing some arithmetic work in a corner while they sat and ate a late supper. Some pickled mackerel as I recall.

'If it was you that betrayed me, Eliza, then I would push out your eyes with my thumbs,' Abe suddenly said, with great vehemence.

'If it was me that did, then those as done for you today

might hear of it and do for you permanent. So place that in your clay pipe and smoke it.'

'Threatened to drive a nail through my knee if ever I touched his tin again.'

'Sssh. Tom'll hear you.'

'Hear on, Tom, for it's to you that I owe this debt. For you.'

'I knew nothing of it, Uncle.'

'Nothing?'

'I swear by . . .' I tried to think what I held most dear. What preoccupied my thoughts and dreams.

'By what?'

'By . . .' I had it. 'By the man in the cloak.'

There was a moment of stark silence in the room, and all I could hear was an onion seller on the pavement beyond the window. Eliza stopped the sewing she held in her hands and looked at her husband, who made no move.

Until he stood up, brows stooping over his eyes like the hood at a Newgate hanging. And then laughed and laughed until tears streamed from his eyes, and he sat down and rested his battered head on the table, roaring his mirth.

'The man in the cloak. Ain't that a rich one, Eliza? Hear what he said? The man . . . the man in . . . in the cloak!'

She joined in the laughter, and so finally did I, though I had no real idea why.

Not then I didn't.

And so the years drifted gently by, until I reached my fourteenth birthday.

CHAPTER FOUR

EDITOR'S NOTE: *There is a great deal more in the Journals of Thomas Goane about his earlier years, but they are full of childish gossip and japes that he played, or that were played on him. There is little of great social interest, as he was privately educated, and therefore mingled with other children to no great degree.*

Nor are there any further references to the 'man in the cloak', which seems strange. He was clearly a boy of quite unusual quickness of mind, and by the time we join him again in 1848 he has progressed.

In more ways than one, I am sorry to say.

For my fourteenth birthday, on the 24th day of September 1848, I was given a fine gold watch. The flash keeper of one of the girls was also a thimble-screwer on the side, and I have no doubt that Uncle Abraham bought it from him. Or obtained it in return for some debt or other.

It was a tumultuous year in Europe. I have in front of me as I write this a notebook in which my teacher urged me to put down all things of interest that happened anywhere in the world. It was a habit that I carried with me in one form or another for the rest of my life.

Let me mention just a few of the events on the Continent, across the Channel, in that one year. In fact, just in those nine months before my birthday. A crucial birthday, as it was to herald the ending of my days as a boy and the beginning of my life as a man.

January. There is a revolt in Sicily against the Bourbons.
February. A revolt in Paris, followed by an abdication

and followed by a Republican government. What revulsion in London over the idea!

March. A revolution in Vienna. A revolt in Venice. A revolt in Milan. Another in Berlin. Yet another in Parma. The niggers rose again in a second Sikh war, after murdering two of our brave lads. And Sardinia declared war on Austria. More than enough to last the whole of a normal year.

April. A revolt in Cracow, and the Austrians are beaten again and again by the Sardinians. The brave Piedmontese, as some called them.

May. Prussia invades Denmark. A revolt in Warsaw, followed by the Communists rising in Paris. A revolt in Vienna. And the collapse of a revolt in Naples.

June. The Austrians are doing better. The summer is damned hot.

July. Revolts in the Danubian Principalities, subdued by the Russians at the request of the Turks. What a tangled mess they are in over there!

August. We have a farthing's worth of trouble from the Dutch in Africa, and beat them soundly. We won't hear any more from them. Not now they've heard how a real British lion sounds when it roars! They are called Boers, but I amuse Aunt Eliza and Uncle Abraham by calling them Bores!

September. I am fourteen!! Hurrah!!

Apart from the watch and the felicitous good wishes from my teacher, there was something else that happened that day which I shall never forget.

But a word of my last teacher is in order. For he was a kinder, better-hearted fellow than many of his predecessors, some of which I used cruelly, as you have read.*

His name was Will Antrobus. A lean, red-haired fellow, who was preoccupied with the sciences and urged me to

* See Editor's Note at beginning of chapter.

follow them, saying they would be the future of our land. He had done much for me in that last year, and I was moved when the honest man gave me a small token of his affection for me. A pretty porcelain statuette of a hawk alighting, which he had brought down from the north after his last visit to his parents, who lived somewhere on the Humber.

I embraced him at our parting, holding him pressed close to me while we mingled our manly tears and wrung each other's hands.

I later returned his wallet to him by a trusted messenger, saying it had been found under a chair. It was a habit that I found hard to cure in myself, though I saw it would bring me naught but harm. After that unhappy incident, I rarely succumbed again.

But my special surprise.

My aunt's house had been doing specially well in the last few weeks, due to her having obtained an attraction that even brought the broughams to our street, and the writers of the ballads had much play with it.

A cock-chafer from Paris. No less. A fine figure of a woman, and I never found out quite what she was doing in a bordello in Seven Dials. But she was marvellous and I fell totally in love with her. I was her adoring slave and I would have done anything in the world for her. She had an enchantingly full figure, and an adorable French accent that I shall make no attempt to duplicate here.

Her name was Nicolette Austée, and I suppose she would have been about twenty. Although she seemed near old enough to be my mother. Not that my mother would have been confused with Nicolette. Not a fair-haired angel like my mother, of spotless purity.

The other girls were jealous of her at first, and I heard more than one whisper in a catty manner that Nicolette was only there to pay off some debt to Uncle Abraham on behalf of her Sicilian protector. It was possible, but I think unlikely. I have met Sicilians before and since, and they have a short way with debts that they do not wish to repay, and it involves the insertion in the victim's mouth of a certain severed part of the anatomy. I will say no more in order to avoid any distress to the gentle sex.

She specialised in what were called 'gentlemen of the back door', though it was still to be some years before I came to understand that phrase. Despite where I was raised, there were still some areas in which I was quite innocent.

Nicolette used to rise about noon, or a little later, and as a 'special' she used to eat with us, giving me three chances each day to admire her in dribbling silence. An admiration that I found produced a strange and new sensation in my body. At times, such as those, I discovered that my trousers had become uncomfortably tight across my John Thomas.

We ate a hearty birthday luncheon, cooked mainly by Eliza herself, with a few close friends from the rookery in. There were eight of us in all, including Mamselle Austée. The food was excellent, fit for the Queen herself.

As the house became busy in the evenings, and all the other guests were creatures of the night, this was the big meal of the day. Supper would be an alfresco affair, with bites snatched between welcoming the regular customers to the house.

One of the doxies wrote a fair hand, and produced for us a real menu of what was to come. Just like in a swells' restaurant.

'On the Fourteenth Birthday of Master Thomas Goane' was what it said, and then it listed what we were to eat. Just to think back on that oak table, creaking beneath the weight of food and drink, makes my mouth to water. Uncle Abe had brought out the best dinner service. Crown Derby it was, in white, with a light brown border. And the crystal glasses glittered in the light of the four-stemmed candelabra. There was so much that the dishes seemed almost to jostle one another for space.

To you reading this so many years after it will probably seem a poor spread, but times were hard for us, and recall that there were only the eight of us.

We began with the soups. Oyster soup or a vermicelli, brimming with vegetables. Almost a meal in itself.

Cods' heads dripping with butter were next, with a deep bowl of fried whiting, crisp and tasty. The main meat course was a saddle of mutton, its fat still spitting and crackling as one of the kitchen maids struggled up the stairs with it.

Curried oysters on the side, for those who were partial to them, as Uncle Abraham was, and a cold collation of pressed meats. Tongue and veal done with olives in the French manner, in honour of my delightful Nicolette. Boiled cabbage, which has never been near the top of my list of favourites, and carrots that are a little better. With a delicious sauce from horse-radishes, hot and spicy, which lay smouldering on the tongue.

The tongue in your head, not the tongue on the table!

Between the eight of us, as it was only a luncheon, there were only six fowls, as well as a fricasseed chicken. There were two ducks, with an orange sauce, and a brace of pheasants, lying in a dish of potatoes, creamed and piped.

One of the fancy coves, called Roaring Paddy, was partial to boiled fowls with an oyster sauce, and Aunt Eliza had provided him with a plump pair, both of which he came near to devouring. There was many a bawdy jest about him nibbling on such a juicy brace of breasts.

Lobster salad brought the meal near to its ending, though few of us partook. And a lemon pudding, with tarts and jellies to complete the repast in fine style. Abe had provided us with a selection of wines, from a warm, sweet port to a watery claret, which he said had rolled off the rear of a wagon near Leadenhall Street just as he was passing.

I was allowed to sip at a brandy, now that I was considered of an age. I didn't let on to them that I had been tasting it for nearly four years, but only in small nips, and topping up the jugs with water so there would be no suspicion.

But I had not drunk it in such proportions before, and it ascended to my head, filling my brain with its heavy fumes.

'I confess, Eliza, to being middling full,' says Roaring Paddy, in the loud voice that gave him his name. A peeler's staff had burst his ears for him years back in a tavern brawl, and he found it hard to judge how his voice sounded to others.

'And I,' chorused the others, and there was a general scraping of chairs and easing of belts and breaches.

Although I am ashamed to admit it, I fear that I was a more than somewhat under the influence of the wine and the brandy. One moment the room was filled with people, and I was having my cheeks bussed by wet lips and hard hands were shaking mine and slapping me on the back. When next I recall anything, the room was nearly empty, though the table still held the rubbish of our meal.

Nearly empty.

Across from me, smoking a small clay pipe, was Nicolette Austée.

'I must have . . .' I stammered, feeling my face flush as red as a monkey's arse.

'You were just sitting there and resting with your eyes shut for a moment. It has been an exciting day, has it not?'

'Yes. It has. But the others . . . ?'

'All gone, my little one. To sleep or to work. To steal or to count their money. There is just you and I who have nothing to do.'

She pronounced it 'nuzzing', and it was the sweetest sound that mortal ears ever heard.

'I must be . . . I suppose that I . . .'

When I tried to stand, the room was switched into a hurdy-gurdy, and I nearly fell. As I stumbled I put my hand on the table. And almost screamed.

It was as though I'd placed my fingers in a wet eye socket. 'It is only the quince jelly,' she laughed.

I wiped my fingers on the cloth, grinning like the fool I felt. How gauche and stupid I was beside this woman of the world. How silly all my dreams of her now appeared to me, face to face. Alone with her.

I had dreamed of this moment, and I had lain in my sweating bed o'nights composing pretty phrases for her that would make her mine.

She watched my face through the coiling tendrils of smoke from her pipe, taking it from her mouth and slowly, very slowly, running a pink tongue over an even row of white teeth.

'You are drunk, my mannikin. And on your birthday. Let me help you.'

'I am not incipict . . . incapacitated.'

But at my next attempt some cad removed the floor from beneath my feet and I tumbled to the carpet, where I lay on my face, laughing at a jest. But I could not remember what it was.

'Has the little fellow banged his little self?' she asked from her chair, in a mocking sort of baby talk.

'Madam,' I said, with all the dignity I could muster from the floor, 'the agony has somewhat abated.'

I heard a chair being pushed back, and it made a most damnable noise, like a hundred hammers being banged on a brass anvil set between my ears. I groaned.

'You are not feeling sick, *cherie*?'

'No. Not sick. But I have an idea that the world has taken to revolving at an unconscionable rate, and I am safest if I remain here.'

'*Mais non,*' said Nicolette. 'That we cannot allow. Let me help you.'

57

I took the chance of opening one eye, and closed it again, as if someone had sprayed hot sand into it. But I heard more movement, so I risked it again. This time the pain was somewhat less.

An inch or so from my right eye I could see the toe of a white satin shoe, with a shapely ankle rising from it, under a curtain of yellow silk. I rolled over on my back and goggled up at Miss Austée, as she bestrode me like some colossus, smiling down at me.

She rested one foot lightly on my chest, and I grabbed it, pressing my hot lips to the satin, feeling the blood rush to my loins at my foolhardy lust. And down below, John Thomas was straining at my trousers. I hoped she wouldn't notice.

She noticed.

Well, after all, she was a whore, and I suppose that it was more or less in her line of business to look for that manner of happening.

'*Mon Dieu*! But what is that Tom Goane?' pulling her foot away and touching me lightly, *there*, with it, so that I groaned, quite losing the last shreds of self-control.

'It's a . . .'

'A what?'

I knew that she was mocking me, but I didn't care. She still stood over me, where I lay helpless on the carpet, and I could see a deal of a way up her dress. Almost to her knee.

'It's a sort of a . . .'

'Perhaps it is . . . how you say it? A leech?'

'Perhaps it is, Nicolette.' Greatly daring to use her first name.

'I hope that great leech of yours will not creep out and bite me. Do you think he might?'

'I wish he might.'

There!

I was dashed if I hadn't said it. Right out. In the open.

Loud and clear. Told her what I wanted.

The times in which I lived were peculiar, and often very confusing. What was thought and what was done were frequently quite different. Much was hidden and secret. In the homes of most folks, everything was guarded and there were many things that were never mentioned. The father of the family would thrash his son for letting slip a careless 'damn' at the dinner table.

Yet that same father might go out of an evening to his club and stop off in the Haymarket to pick up a whore of barely twelve, and swive her until his passions were satisfied. Yet nothing showed on the surface. It was this that was so odd.

Living in Seven Dials, it was impossible not to know what are called the 'facts of life' from an early age. Apart from the dogs that coupled on every street corner, watched by a ring of snot-nosed brats, there was many a family in that square mile who all lived in the same room. And when father came home drunk from the rat-catching and wanted a tumble with his woman, they would rarely even dim the light, and set to in front of the rest of their brood.

I was unlucky in having no sisters to share a bed. If I had been other than a lone orphan, I would have lost my cherry a year or so earlier to one of my own. As it was, I was still a lone virgin, though I had practised that solitary vice that makes men go mad and deaf. I tried to do it sparingly in the hope that I might just become a bit simple and a little hard of hearing.

'Let me help you to your feet, Tom. Give me your hand.'

It was not my hand, gentle reader, that was at the fore of my mind. She had removed her slipper from me, and I had heard a rapping noise which I guessed was her knocking out the shards from her pipe.

Then her shadow fell across me once more, and I lifted my hand to her, marvelling at how heavy it seemed and how devilish long my arm had become. Nicolette leaned over me and tugged, her milk-shop near spilling from the bodice of her dress.

I recall that she was surprisingly strong, and before I knew it I was on my feet, though I was as unsteady as an hour-old calf. Her face was close to mine, and she put her arm under mine to aid me in keeping my balance. She was a wonderfully stunning wench! With a figure that would make a bishop kick over his font.

Something odd happened next, and my mind is blank as to how we left the dining-room and made our way up the back-stairs, the private ones, to my own room. This passing dim-ness of memory is something that I have noticed since when in my cups.

I have no recollection as to where anyone else was, but I must have asked the French filly, as the next thing that re-turned to my memory was Nicolette answering a question of mine.

'Your aunt is out collecting rents with a couple of her bullies, and Abe is gone to Newgate to talk to a turnkey about a flash cracksman.'

Her familiarity with our Seven Dials slang amazed me then, but I must assume that she had spent too long in such society.

'The servants?'

'None that's going to bother us up here, my little bantam.'

I was sitting on my bed, leaning my back against the padded bolster. My feet were bare, and my cravat had been removed. Nicolette also sat on the bed, but near its bottom, her feet tucked up under her, resting one hand on the carved wood of the bed-rail. Smiling gently at me.

'In any case, Tom, I have taken care to lock the door so that nobody can come in and disturb us.'

She dangled the iron key in her hand, and I tried to reach it, but she pulled it back.

'Give me the key, Nicolette. Please. If anyone *should* come...!'

'Very well, naughty boy. I shall hide it, and then you must come seek it.'

And so she dropped it down between her creamy white bosoms, where it vanished clear out of sight.

'Well?'

'What?'

'Do you not want your key?'

'Yes.'

'Well, then?'

'But...'

'But what?'

'I...I don't think I should.'

'Then you are afraid of me?' With a reproachful glance at me under long lashes.

'No.'

Which was a lie. I was more frightened than I had ever been in my life. Because of my special schooling, I was picked upon by the local set of young bullies, who attempted to make me frightened of them. I blacked the eye of one of them and split the lip of another, and I was not bothered again. No, I was not frightened of that sort of action.

'Perhaps I should help you.'

And there and then, in my own bedroom, just as in my most wicked fantasies and dreams, Nicolette Austée, one of the highest-paid biddies in all Finsbury, Marylebone and Westminster, began to peel off her clothes while I lay back and watched her like some African sultan with his favourite dancing girl.

'You like to see this, Tom?'

'Very much.' My tongue seemed to have grown too large for my mouth, and the room had grown damnably stuffy. But the drunkenness had quite vanished, leaving me feeling better than I could ever remember.

'I do this for toffs, and they pay me for each thing I re-move. And they call out to me as at an auction.'

'How?' Aunt Eliza had always done her best to keep me from the rest of the house when they had gentlemen in. Few of them took kindly to a young boy about the place. Now if I had been a young girl . . .

'Item. One pair of shoes.'

I applauded her, a grin hanging by its finger-tips on my lips.

'Item. One pair of stockings. Silk. Slightly torn. That was a bookseller from Long Acre did that last night with his teeth.'

Nicolette was forced to rise from the bed and lift her leg, resting her foot on the mattress close to where I sat, so that I could peruse the shadowy deeps of her gams, clear up to the thighs.

'Item. One petticoat.' A struggle. 'And three more cotton petticoats. And a dress.'

This left her standing grinning at me like a positive imp of mischief, her hands on her hips, wearing only a chemise, and a sort of bodice, and a pair of drawers that were tied round the thighs with pink ribbon.

'Like them, Tom?' she asked, swirling round the room as if she was on the stage.

'They're lovely.' I could not understand why my voice, which had deepened a good six months ago, had chosen this moment to rise to an eldritch squeak.

'Look, They've got what I call a man-trap in them. There!'

I swear that I nearly fainted away like a callow girl. Her drawers, which were of good linen, had an opening in them. At the front. A great slit. Which you could only see when Nicolette stood with her legs apart, thrusting her hips to-wards me. A mound of fluffy, bushy brown hair protruded through the hole in a manner that rather alarmed me, but I remained calm.

As calm as I could.

'Like it? I'll let you touch it in a bit.' *

The next thing that I knew she'd skinned herself of everything except those drawers and was bouncing around on top of the bed. And 'bouncing' is the best word that I can use to describe her. She had monstrous globes, streaked with the finest patchwork lace of pale blue veins.

She took my hand, which I am ashamed to admit was trembling like an old woman with an ague, and pressed my fingers to one, so that I felt the dimpled bit at the end squirm to life like a small animal, springing to attention with the speed of a grenadier. Nicolette chuckled at this, her eyes locking into mine.

'Now you, dearest,' she whispered, her voice hoarse and throaty.

I made no effort to stop her. Indeed, if the Archbishop of Canterbury himself had walked into my bedroom, I think that I should simply have bidden him either to take a seat or to go and sling his hook. There was no turning back.

Within what appeared to be less than a half minute I was as pink and peeled as a shrimp, tucked up under the covers, with John Thomas being handled in a way that I would not have thought possible. I am sure that I was a clumsy tyro, but I bundled away, poking and probing here and there. But mainly 'there', and she wriggled and gasped in French, so at least I may hope she was being pleasured by it.

She used her free hand to guide me, and whispered instructions to me like a Thames waterman bringing in a loaded lighter.

'Up. Down. Harder. Again. Now there. And with *that* just touch me there.'

* After due consultation, I have agreed with the Publisher that most of these scenes should remain in the book, though I have moderated the language here and there. We feel that the modern age is sufficiently enlightened not to be offended.

Despite the yawning chasm at the head of the valley of her drawers, I still found them getting in my way, and I aided Nicolette in untying the ribbons and tugging them free of her loins. Like the best of actors, I believe that a lover should never forget his loins.

Before I knew quite which way was up, we were at the four-legged frolicking, and John Thomas was nosing into the sweetest harbour I had ever looked for. A bosky glen, so cunningly concealed from eyes of man, where I felt that I could play for ever.

For ever lasted a damned short time. I'd hardly hoisted my spinnaker before we were crossing the bar. At the time I gave the mamselle scant attention, being concerned only with wondering if I was dying with pleasure, but she thrashed away like a ferret under a blanket, and clutched me, muttering Frenchie words of encouragement. I hope they were encouragement.

But it was all over too fast.

However, I was able to come-aloft again in good time, and we rolled away the afternoon together in fine style, and I think that I may claim to have acquitted myself as any true English gentleman.

After it was over for the fourth time, Nicolette rolled away from me, and then turned back and smiled. Very gently, and kissed me softly on the lips. A thing that no whore will ever do, and I was conscious of the honour that she thus paid me.

'No more?' asked I, though I confess, dear reader, that there was a strain of boastfulness in me. I doubt that I could have raised a smile for a fifth time, and she knew it.

'No, Tom. My honey-pot fills to o'erflowing, and there is yet much work this night before I can rest.'

'Marry me,' says I, and she shakes her head.

'No. And let us not hear another word between us of what has been your special birthday present from me to you.'

She stood up, yelping as the sheets stuck to her. 'You are a great bear of a lover, Tom Goane, and I am pleased to have had you. But I am so sore. Thank *le Bon Dieu* that my gentlemen tonight are mostly those that prefer the . . . the entrance of the tradesmen.'

I lay still and watched her as she threw on her clothes with practised ease, soaking up the pleasure in what I had done. She saw me smiling at her and blew a kiss, hopping on one leg as she struggled into her drawers.

'It was good?'

'Good?'

'This present?'

'Very.'

'I am pleased.'

'And thank you. I forgot to say it, and I shouldn't. I shall never forget it, Nicolette.' Daring. 'Darling.'

'That is very well. He will be pleased as well that your present was so nice.'

'He?'

'What?' She turned her face away, and I could see that she had spoken without thought and now regretted that she had been indiscreet.

'Who is this "he" you spoke of?'

'Nobody. I must rush.'

'Tell me. Please.'

Nicolette, her breasts still unfettered, came and sat by me, her face suddenly solemn. 'You must promise me that you will never, ever, ever mention what I have said to a living soul. On your life.'

'I promise. Was it the man in the cloak?'

She looked startled, then smiled, seeming relieved. 'That is how you know . . . know him? Yes, it was him. He wanted that you should have a wonderful fourteenth birthday. One you would never forget.'

'It was wonderful.'

'Then I shall tell him, if I ever see him again.'

'Tell him what, Nicolette?' I asked, unable to resist the temptation to tamper with her baby-feeders.

She moved my hand with mock solemnity. 'I shall tell him that I found you a boy.'

'Yes?'

'And I left you a man.'

CHAPTER FIVE

'There's a Judy come from France,
And she leads the toffs a dance,
As they go riding down to Castle Street.
In the pegging-crib she lives,
And her Mary Jane she gives,
While the toffs get a French pig, neat, neat, neat.'

EDITORIAL NOTE: *Though Tom Goane gives no quotes from any of the scurrilous ballads that were printed and sold in such quantities around Seven Dials, I came across this in a small, privately-printed pamphlet dated 1848, so it is just possible that it refers to the lady, Nicolette Austée, who is at the centre of the previous chapter. I hope not, that is if the rhyme is correct, as a 'French pig' was common low slang for a venereal sore.*

I regret that the sordid tone of that chapter is somewhat continued in this next episode, and it is one to which I refer in my Introduction. And I repeat that I do not for one moment believe that the lady in question here is anything other than what Tom says. A lady-in-waiting.

I never saw Nicolette again, and she returned to France shortly after. In the manner of young men of all times, I thought that my heart would break asunder, but it did not, and there were things to do that kept me full busy.

During the next year or so I passed my time in a variety of occupations, none of which give me a great deal of pride when I look back upon them. But I owed a debt to the Levys, and the best way that I could help to repay some of that was by assisting Uncle Abraham in his various enterprises.

I obtained an excellent knowledge of all levels of London life, combined with making the acquaintance of several gentlemen and ladies, both rich and poor, who were to stand me in such good stead at other times in my life.

But I shall not enlarge upon these days, except to mention one incident that will live in my memory until the day that the great publican in the sky comes and tells me to drink up as this is the last round.

The money continued to come in from my mysterious benefactor in the black cloak, and in quantities that increased quarterly, enabling me to dress and equip myself as a young blade about town, though Aunt Eliza, with that eagle's eye of hers, once commented that I looked more like a rake than a blade. A statement that cut me to the very quick, mainly because I saw that there was much truth in it.

But this incident, that I mentioned ...

The year of 1848 was not particularly eventful, apart from a scare when Uncle Abe found it expedient to knock a pursuing constable on the head to dampen his ardour, and the fellow proved to have an uncommonly thin skull. For a few days there was a fine old hue and cry, but the peeler finally recovered his mind and was out of danger, thanks to a speedy piece of work by the sawbones.

Aunt Eliza was also enraged by something that happened on 12th February, when a sum of eighty thousand pounds was voted in to provide a new prison. Outside the city, at Holloway, right up the far end of the Cally Road. And there was talk that it would be for the imprisonment of criminals of the feminine and gentler sex.

Though I know not about the 'gentler sex'. In a house in Mercer Street there lived a female garrotter named Gaping Betty, for a reason that I feel I should not mention, as there may one day be ladies reading my Journals. But Betty stood three inches over six feet, and weighed over twenty stones. It was said that she didn't actually garrotte her victims; she simply broke their necks, but this I doubt, as she was in reality a surprisingly gentle woman.

Though I did see her stop a runaway cab-horse by stepping in front of it and punching it with fearsome ferocity, clean between the eyes, whereupon it fell to its knees.

For wagers she would toss a house brick in the air and hit it with her fist, breaking it into halves.

And there was the birth of another child to our beloved Sovereign. In March, it was little Princess Louise Caroline Alberta. I could not remember whether that was the third or fourth child in the Queen's eight years of marriage. And was not all that surprised to find that the Princess is the *fifth* child.

Albert Edward in 1841. Alice Maud Mary in 1843. Alfred Ernest Albert in 1844. Helena Augusta Victoria in 1846. And now another girl. It may sound disrespectful, but there are those that call Victoria 'the stout brood mare', though I would leap to dispute the 'stout'.

What eminently 'safe' names. Not a Tom among them. Still, with that humourless bore for a father, what can one really expect? Albert Franz August Karl Emmanuel, who is the second – not even the first, mark you – son of the Duke of Saxe-Coburg Gotha.

I have heard from one or two gentlemen that Albert has no sense of humour at all. Except that if you dine with him he will creep round and pull away your chair so that you spill on your backside. And at that he will beat his thighs and his eyes will water at the merriment of it all. I thank God that he is not to be made King.

I must endeavour to avoid my habit of allowing my

Journal to wander into the leafy sidetracks and byways. And press onwards to recount this incident ...

It was some time in July of '48, and it had not rained for a week. Scorching hot weather, bringing everyone out to sit on their roofs and steps. And I also recall that it must have been a Saturday, as Abe refused to work at all on a Saturday, for what he claimed were religious reasons. I had reason to know that he had a better reason. When he claimed to be going to his synagogue, he was actually having a rare old gallop with a filly that he kept in a stable not far from Sloane Street.

It ran for several months, until Aunt Eliza heard of it and put a stop to Uncle Abe's jaunting. I overheard her telling about it to another friend one evening when Abe was out.

'I went and saw the trollop and I told her that I'd fill it up with horse shit and then sew it up for her with cobbler's twine. She scarpered, the dirty biddy. We'll not see her again.'

We didn't.

As I had the afternoon to myself, I elected to go with three or four mates hunting birds' nests and eggs up West. It had become a game with us to try to find a garden that was closely guarded and then steal in and run off with proof of our daring.

Each time we aimed higher and harder, going for the houses of the quality. The previous week the old Duke of Wellington himself near as a toucher caught us in his town house trees. If the old boy had been a flea's wing more spry it would have gone hard. But it was this that added a spice of danger to our young boys' dish.

There were five of us in all, as started off from the rookery. But Jemmy was collared by his ma and made to stand watch over their new baby. That left four.

And me the eldest and the leader of them, by way of being

stronger. This meant also that I needs must be the first in daring.

Just as we were leaving Castle Street, Benny Stein's ma calls him from her window. 'Go to your Aunt Ruth's and get the latkes for supper, and don't forget the onions. And you didn't eat up your cholent this morning. Are you ailing or something? Come here and put on a warmer jacket, Benny. Better yet, come in and don't go out with those boys.'

That left three, so we sallied away from Seven Dials, waving farewell to poor Benny and his grumble-gizzard of a ma.

Along Gerrard Street, down Rupert Street and then along Coventry Street, past the top end of the Haymarket, where some of Aunt Eliza's girls went of an evening to pick up their custom.

Two hansoms had locked wheels on the corner of Piccadilly and Duke Street, so we stayed there and enjoyed the excitement. Both drivers were off their perches and were squaring up to each other, while a ring gathered round, urging them on. But the toff who was riding in one of the cabs stepped down and dusted them both off in a sharp manner.

The two boys with me were brothers, called Charley and Isaiah Dorning. Isaiah was the younger, and he had a most fearful squint, which helped him work as a dip around the public houses. The gulls never knew whether he was eyeing their wallets or the sky. It was said that when he was born he lay there in his cradle, squint-a-pipes to all the world, and his pa asked what he was to be called, and his ma replied it had better by 'Isaiah', as she said 'one eye's 'igher than the other'.

Both helped out a couple of fruit costers some days, and both wore their velveteen breeches, and the long corduroy coats common to their type, with flashy brass buttons. Charley was proud as could be of his bright new kingsman handkerchief, with a blue pigeon's eye design on it in silk, sporting it knotted loosely at this throat.

'Where we goin' to go?' asked Isaiah, rolling one eye along Piccadilly and the other down St James's.

I led the way along the back of the Palace, down Queen's Walk and into the Mall, not far from *the* Palace. Uncle Abe remembered it when it was called 'King's Palace', but now all knew it as Buckingham Palace, and it was there that our dear monarch spent much of her time while in the capital, though it was whispered that she was happier when at Balmoral or one of the other royal homes. Still, today the flag fluttered, showing she was in residence. And that flag gave me an idea for our most daring adventure yet.

'There,' I said, loping off, followed by the Dorning brothers.

'Where we goin'?' asked Charley, looking round suspiciously at the smartly dressed crowds that paraded up and down in front of the Palace.

'In there,' I says, dodging a squadron of Life Guards coming clattering along the cobbles, damn near sending us spinning in the gutter.

'There!?' cries out Isaiah, his voice sounding like a saw drawn along a sheet of glass in his amazement.

I grinned. It was good for my position as a leader to be able to shock those under me. That was what an officer told me at my aunt's one night. It was a great truth, and it stuck in my mind. I recall that this same man carried a small pistol in a holster under his arm, and I asked him why he felt he needed a weapon at such a time.

'It is better, young Tom Goane, to be carrying a pistol and not need it than to need a pistol and not be carrying it.'

There have been times that I have known well what he meant by that.

'Yes,' I replied. 'We shall go into the grounds of the Palace itself and steal us some eggs there. That will be a fine game for a Saturday.'

There was a silence between us, and I saw that I had

o'erstepped the mark with them. And I felt a sudden chill feather my spine, like a whore's fingers spider-clawing at you, as I thought of the danger of what I purposed.

'You've gorn cracked, Tom Goane. All that bleedin' schoolin'! It's made you right round the bleedin' bend.'

'You wouldn't be having a touch of the belly-wobbles, would you?'

His fist clenched, and out of the corner of my eye I noticed his brother moving edgily around me. 'No cove like you says that to me. Not even you, Tom.'

'If the cap fits, Charley Dorning, then you wear it. And,' spinning round to face Isaiah, 'I'll spread your beaky nose all over your face, Ike, if you try your sneaking ways round me!'

For a moment, I thought that they might both attack me, but they knew me, and I knew them. I had been taught to defend myself by an old pug who'd once fought the Dulwich Gypsy and I knew enough of how to handle my dukes in a bundle to make them wary of me.

'Well, Tom. We'll be soddin' orf now, and if you ever gets out of there with your skin in one piece, then come and show us the eggs you get.'

'I'll place a bob on it, Charley.'

Both their faces looked doubtful. Isaiah sniffed, wiping his nose with his kingsman. 'We see you go in and come out?'

'Course. Is it a wager?'

'Yes. It is. And we'll come down to the river to watch you sail orf with the convicts in a month or so after the Assize ships you to Australia.'

So we shook hands like the nobs over a thousand guineas, though we all knew that it was no great joke about the risk of being transported. Indeed, I was not sure for myself that if I was caught raiding the grounds of Buckingham Palace

I might not face being topped on a Monday morning outside Newgate.

They came with me around the north side of the gardens, with Green Park a wooded space on the other flank of Constitution Hill. The sun was well up, and the pavements were filling up each minute with more of London promenading in the summer air.

There was a place where a tree stood close to the wall, and we paused there, looking both ways to make sure there was no sign of any guards or peelers.

'All clear,' said Charley.

But there were the passers-by to worry about. If any of them saw a strapping lad of fourteen, and looking more than my age, vaulting into the grounds of the Palace, then there would be such an outcry as has never been heard, and I would be as helpless as a Smithfield bullock.

But the Dornings were stout mates, and they did the trick for me. By staging a fight on the edge of the roadway, which attracted a crowd in seconds.

'Your mother's a spigot-suckin' old bag!' yelled out Charley.

'And yours is a tuppenny bunk-up in Billingsgate,' replied Isaiah.

The punches flew thick and fast, and I was left against the wall, with only a ring of backs and bustles to look at. It took me a moment to shin up the tree and along a low branch, well hidden by the rich foliage. Ahead of me I saw the top of the Palace wall, and beyond that I could see the thick trees of the gardens and, gleaming among the leaves, the water of the lake.

The noise faded behind me as I dropped silently down, bending my knees to make an easy landing. My eyes flicked from side to side like a sharper at a police party, looking for any sign of sentries. For I had no way of ascertaining what sort of a reception I might find there. It might have been a bayonet through the guts for me. But it was all as silent as a plague pit at midnight.

There were all manner of trees there, and I cautiously crept from trunk to trunk, always watching around me, making me fearful even of my own shadow. A narrow path showed away to my right and I took it, keeping to one side, ready to leap for my life.

I wasn't sure what sort of proof I might find there to prove what I had done, as it was late in the year for any eggs. But I was full of hope that something would come along. It nearly always did.

And it did.

But it wasn't what I wanted. All that I looked for was a quiet spot buried among some shrubbery where I could seek out a nest or find some other sort of proof that I hadn't just hopped over the wall, waited a few minutes and then scarpered back again like a leech with salt on its tail.

But what I got was a flurry of activity further along the pathway, and the sound of giggling voices and men shouting. I heard the rustle of skirts, and feet tripping along towards me, from round a corner, beyond a moss-covered sundial.

I decided that the best course of action was one that would remove me from the oncoming people, so I dived unceremoniously into the thicket, landing on my stomach in a small sunken garden with a whoosh that quite took all the breath from my body.

By the time that I had somewhat recovered both my breath and my dignity, the voices were very close. I guessed that it was some members of the royal household playing a game of hide-go-seek. Probably footmen and maids using their free time for a frolic. Having gone for too long after my adventures with the mamselle, I would not have been averse to a frolic myself, had the opportunity presented itself to me.

'I am getting warm,' shouted a voice. A man. Very nobby for a servant. Perhaps it was the ladies and gentlemen of the bedchamber, or whatever they called those very high-up and special servants.

'Oooh.'

It was like the frightened squeak of a mouse, just through the thick screen of bushes on the path that I had so hastily left. A woman. Young by the voice.

I lay back in a bed of small scrubby flowers. A pale yellow in colour, with prickly stems. All I could do was hope and trust in the Lord that I would be able to remain hidden. By the state of the part of the gardens where I was lurking not even a conscientious under-gardener had been there for many a long year.

Unless I was damnably unlucky I would be able to remain hidden there while the game went by.

It will not surprise you to know that luck is one commodity that the Goane market often lacks.

The bushes that had only just straightened behind me now bent double again, and someone came catapulting through them, gasping fit to bust, then tripped over a tangling bramble and fell in a heap right at my feet.

You will, I am sure, forgive me for the momentary thought that the best course of action would be a swift blow to the back of the neck and a hurried retreat. Not just out of the grounds of Buckingham Palace, but all the way back to the safety of the rookery in Seven Dials. And then under the blankets.

'Oh dear. Sir John. You have taken me most fairly and most squarely, and I will . . .'

Then she looked up.

'Who the . . . You are not Sir John.'

Whoever this lady was, I had to allow a full set of honours for her perception. She had noticed that I was not this mysterious 'Sir John', whoever he might be. I was supposing that she was not making a reference to my own Sir John, who was, in any case, remaining well hidden.

There was a silence, bursting with a most fearful tension. The lady sat up, brushing her skirt down with both hands as she did so, her eyes never leaving my face. There was a strange dignity to her, until she belched. Loudly, like a cork popping from a cask of small beer.

Now I would challenge anyone to remain on their dignity having done that. Specially in the presence of a complete stranger. And this lady was no exception to that rule.

'I do beg your pardon, Sir John. But I have never in my life drunk that cider. It is very strong, Sir John. Oh, but I am forgetting. You are not Sir John Dalhousie, are you? Are you?'

The repeated question cracked like a whip, which made me doubt for a moment that the lady was indeed a servant, but one would hardly find . . . well, anyone else lying as drunk as a lord—or lady—in the shrubbery of Buckingham Palace.

'My name is Tom Goane.'

'Is there not something that you have forgotten, Mister Goane?'

'I don't think so.'

A look of some bewilderment passed her face, and she attempted to rise, being defeated by a lack of strength in her knees, and she sat down again with a most undignified bump on her round little bottom. Not perhaps all *that* little, but pretty enough to my hungry eyes.

'What were we talking of, Mister . . . ?'

'Goane. Thomas Goane.'

'Quite. Are you playing in this game of catch the hindmost, Mister . . . ?'

'I'm Goane.'

'Oh. Must you, and we've only just met?'

'Not "going". Goane. Tom.'

'Young Tom. You're a pretty fellow, Tom. Really very handsome.'

I had been thinking that the lady was not lacking in being a bit of a stunner herself. Not a lot of a stunner, you understand.

She seemed inclined to shortness, but as I had hardly seen her on her feet it was not easy to judge. Her dress was marvellous. Even by the standards of the greatest court in the civilised world. Pale pink silk, as watery and weak as a Thames sunset through a mist. Embroidered with a whole meadowful of white and yellow flowers.

High over the bodice, where I observed that her baby's public house was in good order. Ruffled sleeves, shot with a darker shade of red. But still scarcely bright enough to merit the name of red. Her shoes were black, with only a plain buckle of silver. As she fell I noticed that the soles of her shoes were hardly scuffed, as thought she'd just put them on that morning. Or as though she were not used to walking any distance out of doors.

'You are staring at me in what I cannot but observe is rather a rude and impertinent manner.'

There it was again, That imperious tone. Perhaps she was used to giving orders to a fleet of servants. Mistress of the Household, or some such title.

'My apologies, ma'am.' Though she seemed only in her late twenties, she appeared to like a bit of respect. 'But I confess to staring at you. In the same way that I would stare at a great painting.'

She smiled. 'I forgive you. And I am used to being stared at.'

Conceited minx!

Her face was a little flattish and moon-like, with smallish eyes set too close together for my tastes. Her hair was not a crowning glory, being indeterminate in colour, pulled back in a severe manner and parted down the middle, which I thought served mainly to draw attention to her over-high forehead. Her mouth was pretty and her smile radiant.

And the sun was shining, and the noise of her chasing companions had vanished away in to the distance, disappearing towards the lake. And I was near fifteen, feeling almost drunk with the elation of the danger of my own position in such a forbidden place with such a lady. It would have turned the head of any youth.

'Are you used to being kissed, ma'am?' I asked her, greatly daring.

'Aaah! I do so enjoy riddles and conundrums. You clever boy!'

I was taken all aback by that answer.

'I mean to ask you whether you truly enjoy being kissed?'

'It is not a riddle?' There was a rapid and distinct chill fallen across the clearing where we sat, huddled together so close that I could reach out and touch her hand.

I reached out and touched her hand.

During our conversation over the next ten minutes or so the lady revealed that she had never ever imbibed cider before and that she had not the slightest intention of doing so again, remarking that it made her feel beastly sick.

Though 'beastly' is not the word that she used, being a real lady and all.

But in other things she was no different from any Castle Street palliasse. When she kissed me, after demurring for a longish time, I was close to jetting my juice over her for her lips were just as they should be.

And after that . . .

Well, we talked of this and that.*

* It is at this point that I have my strongest suspicions about Tom Goane's honesty and frankness. At all other points in his Journals he is quite open. Yet here, he becomes almost coy about what he and this unnamed lady did in the shrubbery. Perhaps it was less than he

79

And she was not unwilling to most sports, though often pausing to complain that she was not well. Once I feared she was about to throw the cat's all over me, and I pulled away, but she controlled herself.

Just as we were reaching the most interesting part of our converse, we were interrupted. The lady was just moaning that she was a married lady and a mother, and then turning again to our own game with renewed vigour, when we heard a voice calling out somewhere away to our right.

'Are you zere? Hello! Hello!'

I froze. The real danger of my position came back to me again, with a renewed force. To be caught in the act. Not quite *in* the act, gentle reader, but as near as makes short odds. In the Palace grounds with . . . such a lady. Who might recover from her quite unique intoxication and call out that she had been ravished.

Near as a toucher I swooned away at the thought of what kind of punishment might be reserved for such a heinous sin.

'Hello! Are you zere? Iz sometink wrong?'

The accent was heavily Germanic.

'I must be going,' says I, rising to my feet, disentangling myself from her in a somewhat ungentlemanly manner, but needs must when what sounds like a husband arrives.

'It is I, my sveetheart. Haff you become unvell? Vere are you?'

The voice was getting closer and louder, and the lady in question was also beginning to show distressing signs that she was becoming aware of her position. Which was flat on her back in the shrubbery with her clothing in what might be considered by some to be disarray.

---

had hoped. Or possibly he is being tactful to conceal from us the true identity of the lady in question. I leave the answer to you, the reader.

There was a length of ribbon in my hand from the neck of her dress and I pondered for a moment whether I should try to place it back in again. But once you have taken it out, then it is often harder to replace it. Specially when, like this ribbon, it has become rather limp. And it would have taken me an age simply to thread it through the hole.

So it was time for my goodbyes.

'I have greatly enjoyed meeting you.'

'But . . .'

'I'm going, ma'am.'

'Yes. I do recall your name, Mister Goane. Never fear of that.'

There were other voices in the hunt, and the bushes around were being beaten as though they were after a whole pack of partridges instead of one short lady in a pale pink dress.

By sliding off the the left and cutting back to the wall, I was able to make safety, though there was a deal of hueing and crying going on behind me.

The Dorning brothers had vanished, but I dropped over the wall, nearly landing on a prosperous gent and his eight children, taking a constitutional up Constitution Hill, and causing his stout wife to faint away.

In the confusion I made good my escape, eventually catching up with Charley and Ike not far from the end of the Mall. Having waited near an hour for me, they had attracted the attention of a peeler and beat a retreat before prisoners were taken.

They asked for me to show where my proof was of the birds, but my plucking had been of a different order. Although I was greatly tempted to reveal all, or nearly all, I am still a gentleman at heart, and I pretended that I had been damn near nicked and parted with a bob, considering that I had been given fine value for my money.

For had I not a piece of quality ribbon tucked in the

right-hand pocket of my jacket? And a taste on my mouth that didn't all come from my own lips?

I remembered that lady for many a day, and I can still see her face even now, as I sit here writing. A pretty face, and friendly, though admittedly somewhat in drink. And yet as I left her with such haste, I recall one thing about her that no man could deny.

As I made my hasty departure, I glanced back. And she was clearly not amused.

CHAPTER SIX

'One lad that I spoke to on several occasions was of the greatest assistance to me in my studies. He was rising fifteen, but big and strong for his age. Well-dressed in clothes of some modesty. Unusual in that part of London. Unlike many boys of his age in and around the vicinity of Seven Dials his face was open and frank. A likeable and friendly countenance, without the pinched foxy look of most of the thieves and criminals in those parts.

'I asked him if he would assist me, and he did so, telling me that he lived with his guardians, and that his aunt ran a bordello and his uncle—a Hebrew—was in and out of many species of dishonest activity, but he assured me that there was "no vindictiveness in him".

'The boy, whose name was Tom, was also unusual in that he was well educated. Better than the eldest sons of many of our finest families. This was, I think, in part due to the fact that he clearly possessed a wonderfully developed natural wit. And partly from the fact that he told me he was in receipt of a secret income from a mysterious benefactor.

'I was at a loss to ascertain precisely how he passed his time and earned any money for himself, and he told me that he had great expectations, and hoped to mix with the high and the mighty, and ultimately to travel and see the world.

'Tom was a quite remarkable boy, and I have often wished that it had been possible to keep close to him and discover how he ended his days. Without him as a guide and translator, much of my work among the labouring and under-

world classes of London during the late 1840s would all have
been much hindered.'

*From Unpublished Papers
of Social Research,
attributed by some to Henry
Mayhew, author and
sociologist.*

EDITORIAL NOTE: *I came across the document above while
researching into background material to corroborate
Thomas Goane's Journals, and I reproduce it here as something of interest to the next chapter. I personally doubt that
it is actually by Henry Mayhew himself, though it may have
been written by one of his army of assistants and researchers.
Yet, from this next chapter, there seems little doubt that
Mayhew did meet Tom, and the evidence from the passage
above is strong, though circumstantial. As in other matters,
I leave it to the judgement of you, the reader.*

He was a funny-looking cove.

It was a hard winter, was '48. Ice on all the gutters and
snow lying on the roofs thicker than crackling on a fat chop.
Uncle Abe had slipped on the ice while carrying out his
studies of the materials used in roofing and had been helped
home to our house by two of his friends, who simply de-
posited him on the step and sloped off, after ringing the bell.

With him on his back with a splinted leg, the flow of
money into the Levy coffers ceased as abruptly as turning off
the tap on a cask of port. Aunt Eliza was doing well from
the girls, but there had been pressure by some doddering old
biddies who wanted what they called the 'great wen of Seven
Dials' to be lanced open and the 'noxious poison drained
away for ever'.

Nosy old beggars!

But all this botheration meant that a few of the good

solid fathers of the families had their consciences tapped and held off from the bawdy-houses for a few weeks.

What all this amounted to was that young Tom had to go out and find work.

As it turned out, the work came and found me.

I had scarcely left our rookery when I saw the signs of a disturbance at the end of the road, not far from the open space of the actual junction of Seven Dials. There was a group of rowdies circling a gent. Stout sort of a fellow, with a grey frock coat and a high hat, which was knocked off his head as I watched.

'I tell you, I am not a policeman,' he was shouting out, and I closed in, wondering if he might, accidentally-like, drop his wallet or a watch or a wipe.

'Kick the sneakin' bugger's 'ead in!' shouted one man, and the cry was taken up by others.

Now Tom Goane is all for a bit of a sport, and any man like him who was fool enough to walk in our area without a couple of bullies to protect him deserved anything he got, and I might have been one of the first to heave a half-brick at him. But this was different. And ugly. The men around him were largely the out-of-work and the drunks, who ponced off whores for enough tin to keep them semi-sensible in ale. There wasn't an honest villain there, with a few brats hanging barefoot around, one of them prising up a lump of frozen dung and chucking it at the toff, striking him on the shoulder, bringing a cheer from the circling crowd.

'Please! I beg of you. I am here to try to help, and I will pay for aid and information.'

He was a brave chap, there alone, not seeming to realise how dangerous his position was. There were enough culverts and covered streams in London then for a few slit corpses to disappear and no questions. I have seen it happen.

But I had caught the word 'pay', and that was for me.

But to get at it, I had first to rescue the gentleman from a mob that was becoming more unpleasant by the second.

In a moment he would be rolling in the ice, with iron-capped boots puddling his brains.

'Peelers!'

It was enough, as I knew it would be.

Snot-nose children in the rookeries often risked adult anger by shouting out a spurious warning, but nobody ever took the chance.

The street was deserted faster than a Froggy retreat, leaving the old gentleman standing quite alone, looking round in bewilderment, stooping to pick up his hat and dust it down, absently rubbing at the patch on his smart coat where the dung had hit him.

'All right, governor?' I said, moving in close to him, so that he would realise that it had been me who had saved his mutton for him.

'Yes, Thank you, young man. I am in your debt, I imagine? Am I not?'

'Middling so, sir. Had I not sent them running, those rats would have had you down and robbed in two shakes of a gnat's tail.'

'Ah. What a picturesque expression. I must note it down. Was it two shakes of a flea's tail?'

'A gnat's tail, sir.'

I stood patiently waiting while he scribbled something in a small, morocco-bound notebook, with rings at the top that held a neat gold pencil.

'There. Thank you, Mister...?'

'Goane. Thomas Goane, sir. Can I be of any further assistance to you?'

'Yes. I believe you can. My name is Mayhew. Henry Mayhew. And I am writing a book.'

'Like Charles Dickens?'

He laughed. I saw that he was a jolly man, with a rounded

face and a surfeit of chins, all a'wobble as he shook with merriment. While he laughed we walked, and while we walked we talked. And that walk and talk went on, in the end, for several weeks.

Many of my adventures were quite wonderful, and I found him one of the most marvellous men I had ever met, giving me new hope and ambition to improve on my own lowly station in life. He told me of things I had never dreamed of, and in return I told him all I could about London. Not the top side of the city, which most Putney clerks know. But my London.

'It's like turning over a great golden stone, Tom,' he once said to me, 'and finding that its underneath is slimy and covered in rot and decay.'

His book was to be called *London Labour and the London Poor*, and something new it will be when it appears. If ever it chances that you can get hold of one, either by begging or by borrowing or by buying—even by stealing if you must— then do so.

For a big fellow he was wonderfully soft of heart, and I have seen him weeping as he took his notes in that little book of his, as some orphan in rags told him their sorry tale.

'So many children, Tom,' he said. 'It is not the men and women for whom I shed my tears. But I suffer for the little children.' In Seven Dials alone, he thought that were several thousand workhouse runners. Children sometimes as young as six or seven who had scarpered from the local work-houses.

Not that I blamed them for cutting out. I had a friend, taken by typhoid in '47, who had lived for a year and a half in such a place. He spent his days picking oakum and his nights in a huge, cold, bare dormitory with a hundred other boys under a vast painted message which said, 'The lower orders must be kept in a state of poverty, or they will never be stimulated to be industrious.'

And the food!

Breakfast was a bowl of gruel made from cornmeal or oatmeal. By now I had begun to read what I could when I could, and I had devoured *Oliver Twist* with the keenest pleasure. Anyone would have heartfelt sympathy for poor Oliver wanting some more. Even of that tasteless slop.

A quarter pound of bread, and half that amount of cheese each day, with a half pound of potatoes, all wormy and green. Occasionally some maggot-crawling meat or some greasy broth. And as a treat there might be either suet or rice pudding a couple of times each week.

This wasn't what Henry Mayhew hated so much. It was what it caused in the cities. And specially in London. One time he was surrounded by begging children and made to pull out a purse and give them what small change he had, but I checked him, knowing that we would both be bidding fair to be torn apart.

It was down near one of the worst of the infested rookeries in all London. Down at Rotherhithe, at a place called Jacob's Island.

Near the end of a freezing February in '49. It was the time that Uncle Abe was getting up and about once more and crowing his glee from the tops of the bridges at the news that Benjamin Disraeli had been elected to the leadership of the Conservatives.

'One of our boys!' was Uncle Abraham's expression, though I doubt that Disraeli would have claimed that degree of kinship with Abe Levy.

Earlier we had talked to one of the toshers, recovering from being bitten on the thigh by a rat while he delved among the sewers under the city. There were those who envied the toshers, for they often came across valuable finds among the filth, but it would not be an occupation for me. There was a better than middling risk of being trapped down there and drowned in the muck.

Mister Mayhew was appalled that any man should be forced to thus earn his tin, but the tosher was quite happy in his work. I think that if I had the choice I would prefer that to the pure-finders, who trailed the pavements following dogs. Each man or woman or child had a small shovel with which they lifted the droppings and carried them to the local tannery.

I have sunk low in my time, but never so low as that.

'I would visit a bordello, and speak to the woman who runs it and to one of the girls. Can this be easily arranged, Tom?' asks Mister Mayhew, a bit of a twinkle in his eyes.

'I'm game enough.'

'Perhaps your aunt's establishment?'

'No. Perhaps not, Mister Mayhew. I warrant that Aunt Eliza would not wish to see her house in your book, else there's trouble from the peelers. She pays them a remittance as it is to leave her alone, as do all the keepers. But we are close on to Red Carole's.'

'Excellent. But is there a cheap eating-house on our way? I am feeling that the inner man is in need of some sort of refreshment.'

'There's nothing fine enough for you.'

I privately hoped that Mister Mayhew would take me with him to one of the nobs' eating-places, as I was developing a taste for good food. The previous day, with the wind set in the east raw enough to freeze the flesh off a mortified monk, we had adjourned into Dolly's Chop House in the Churchyard of St Paul's. A most superior example of its type, as Mister Mayhew noted in his book. Apart from taking down every word that folks say, he also scribbled down what they wear and what they eat and drink, and on and on and on until I fear his pencil will burst a'flame. I need no pencil, as I am blessed with a memory that remembers all and forgets naught.

That lunch we ate, to prove that my boast is not an idle one, a pair of chops each, fine and thick as a collier's fist, grilled over a charcoal fire with pickled walnuts. Bread and beer and wow-wow sauce, spiced up with capers and horse-radish vinegar. Mister Mayhew was a sturdy trencherman and also managed to plough his way through a brimming bowl of buttered potatoes.

But not today.

'I want somewhere where we can sit in a corner and ob-serve without being taken for either priests or policemen, Tom. And as damnably cheap as you can get.'

Red Carole's was only a stone's throw away from us, near the corner of Queen Street. But on the way was a rambling and smoking place where the sweepers in particular ate. Ned the Fisher's it was called, named after its lantern-jawed owner, who had obtained his capital by a ruse involving a fishing rod and lurking on bridges, becoming quite well known in his special sphere.

The food was terrible, and only the four shillings a day that Mister Mayhew paid me kept me there. The only pal-atable thing was some porter that I happened to know had been snitched off a wagon unloading outside Boodles Club the previous night. I shall keep my lips sealed as to how that item of information came into my possession.

We both ate their tuppenny-ha'penny special. I shudder to try to imagine what their penny ordinary can have been like. Mister Mayhew and I were served, if served is the right word for two filthy plates brimming with watery gravy being dumped in front of us, with one small saveloy and wormy potatoes and soggy cabbage, followed by a thin scrap of pudding. We were unable to guess what type of a pudding it was and my host asked Ned if he knew.

'What manner of pudding?'

'Yes.'

'The pudding?'

'Precisely. You have grasped the very root of my question. It's nub, as it were. What manner of pudding is this?'

'Why, it's the tuppenny-ha'penny pudding, governor, and if you like it not, then you may take it in both hands and ram it up your arse!'

Mister Mayhew said that the quality of the food reminded him of his public school. Specially the cabbage.

Red Carole was delighted to see me, and glad that I'd brought her a gull. As she thought, but she was less happy when I informed her that my friend wished only to talk.

'Will he pay for that?'

'Aye. And wishes that he and I talk to you and one of your girls at the same time.'

Carole looked at me all askance, her head on one side as she pondered on this one. She was a devilish pretty woman, despite running one of the hardest houses in all London. Aunt Eliza had once seen her take on three drunken sailors and beat them all from her house, using only the sharp edge of her tongue And the sharper edge of an open razor that she carried in a leather pouch slung between her hemispheres.

She had flaming red hair, which cascaded over her shoulders in tumbling ringlets. And she always lived up to her nickname by wearing a red dress and red shoes.

'Do you mean the poor sod can't get it up without we all sit around and talk?'

Her eyes opened wide, and she shook her head. 'And him a fine figure of a man, though spreading somewhat around the middle like a jeroboam of wind.'

I still do not know why my personal imp of mischief chose that moment to take possession of me, for I liked Henry Mayhew and greatly admired him for his humanity. But there was something in him that I could not fully fathom. I stood by and listened as he catechised the most outrageous drabs in Wapping, and yet never saw him roused by their presence. But there was a gleam to his eye, as a man who would do more were his coat not so tight and his stock so constricting. And so it came to me that I might both have a jest and aid him in loosening that stock somewhat.

He had paid me well, but time was slipping by me, and spring was not that far away. It was, so I thought, as good a moment as any to be moving on.

So I took Carole on one side and whispered in her ear, so that she shook with laughing and jigged about so that her titties bounced to and fro in a most captivating manner.

'But who'll pay for it?'

'Why not you? You love a jest as well as any, and I've steered a few passengers to your carriage before now and no questions asked.'

She nodded. 'That's fair and upright, Tommy Goane. And by Venus, but I'll do it.'

Mister Mayhew sat stolidly on in a corner where I'd put him, eyeing up the harlots as they passed in front of him, quite ignoring him until they were tipped the wink by Red Carole. Clicking along in her high-heeled red shoes, she went off up the narrow staircase and reappeared moments later with her arm across the shoulders of another frow that I knew well.

She was as skinny as a spider-catcher and was known as Thin Mary. She had moved to Red Carole's crib from another place up West after a disagreement with her keeper there over tin. I believe that at that time there was a warrant out against her for pouring boiling water over the fellow's private parts and running off with his money. But that was under her other name of White Josie.

Mary came over to me, grinning like a cat that's had the cream. 'You want us to help that old man have his supper, is that it, Tom?'

'Aye. And I'll tip you a couple of bob if you can get him peeled like a prawn within one minute of having him up those stairs.'

Carole went over to the door and spoke to the giant black who was her chucker, warning him that she would be busy for a few minutes; then she smiles at me and pulls me a slanting wink out of her weather eye, away from poor Mister Mayhew, who is still scratching away in his book and staring pop-eyed at a mulatto wench wearing only a pair of shoes and feathered neckerchief.

'Sir?'

'What?'

'Young Tom here says as how you're looking for some private conversation. With me and Thin Mary here. Will we do for you?'

Henry, ever the gentleman, stands up and bows, which throws all the girls into giggling, and one of them drops a glass of gin she's sipping in one corner.

Carole plays up to him and drops him a deep curtsey, revealing even more of her jugs, so that his eyes start out like mission organ stops. Thin Mary stands watching, absently picking her nose, and Carole turns to her, a sweet smile glued in place.

'Drop a curtsey to the toff, there's a good girl.' And without changing the tone of her voice, 'Or I'll slice off your ears and feed them to you pickled.'

So Thin Mary also curtseys, lifting her skirt so high in doing so that she reveals she is, like most of the other troopers, wearing no drawers.

I have to turn away to the wall and make the pretence that I am overwhelmed by a choking fit, for the sight of Mayhew's physog, which has gone as purple as a plum, and his eyes like cherries stuck in a compote.

'Will . . . will you come up with us, then, Tom?' asks

Mister M. and I nods away and tugs at my forelock, like the best crossing sweeper or link-boy.

'Be right there, Mister Mayhew. But I must first make my way out to the jakes and plant a sweet pea, if I can find my path through this damned London particular.'

For a real souper had sprung up, threading in and out of the narrow streets and alleys like a rich man's winding scarf. I slipped out through the rear door, past the small discipline room, where I could hear the slaps and cries of a session well on its way towards a red bum and golden guinea.

By the time I returned, the two women were shepherding my governor—soon to be my ex-governor—up the stairs towards one of the rooms opening off the narrow landing. All the walls were done out in red plush, which cost Carole a pretty penny. Or it would have done had it not all been supplied by a gent who runs a large establishment up West, and he let her have it free in return for certain favours.

The last I saw of the great Henry Mayhew was his silk hat disappearing out of sight. He would insist on wearing that even in the roughest parts of Hoxton and Hackney, though I had done what I could to coax him from the habit. With a final fling of her skirt and red shoes, Carole and Thin Mary vanished and the door was shut. The room downstairs where I stood had fallen silent, and we all heard the unmistakable click of a key turning in a lock.

It was nearly the hour when I should be departing, but I could no more leave until the last card was dealt than I could have flown up to the moon. So I sat me down in a velvet armchair with a creaky leg, and toyed with the bare bottom of one of the girls, and listened, as did all the others. I can still see the white teeth of her chucker gleaming in delight in his great black face.

There was nothing, and I was beginning to get concerned less something should have gone amiss with my strategem. It dragged on for so long that I was considering spending a few bob and slipping upstairs and polishing my arse on the top sheet with the mulatto.

Then there was a hoarse cry, like when a man awakes from a sleep in the park and finds the pigeons have left their calling cards on his best waistcoat. A battering on the door, and then more screams and shouts. The black moved from the entrance, standing by the stairs, grinning at me, but the smile was not reflected in his rolling eyes and his fingers toyed with a narrow-bladed butcher's knife.

Then the door opens at the top, and Red Carole sticks out a head. 'All clear, boys,' she shouted. 'Here's some togs for you to keep watch on. He'll not be wanting them for a while.'

And she heaved down to us a great pile of apparel. With a shining silk hat on top of it.

'Damnation, madam!' I heard a great voice that I knew to be Mister Mayhew. 'Unhand me or I call for the peelers. Young Tom! Ho there!'

'Don't worry so, governor!' I shouted. 'No harm'll come. Like they say. If it's unavoidable that you are to be ravished, then lie back and think of your country.'

I didn't hear his reply.

'Grab his knees, Mary!' I heard next.

'Ooooh! No. Madam!'

'Sit on his head. That'll shut him up for a bit and give him something to bite on.'

'Better than a bullet!' calls up one of the biddies from downstairs.

'Not if it's Thin Mary's!' shouts another. 'Her arse is as bony as a coster's donkey.'

A shoe comes flying through the open door, bouncing on the carpet not a yard from where I'm sitting. It's a red satin shoe with a high heel.

It's a well known fact around Seven Dials that her shoes are the very last thing that Red Carole takes off before settling down to work, so I know that I'm leaving Mister Mayhew in the best of hands. Though I am inclined to the belief, from the muffled noises we can hear, that it's not their hands they're using.

And so I waved a fond farewell to the crib, feeling as I stepped into the pitchy fog that I had done what Mister Mayhew ordered. He had told me he wanted to get to the bottom of the bordello trade, and that was precisely where I had left him!

I enjoy walking in a fog, and there's always something to hear and chances for a bright lad to make his fortune. In that sort of weather, folks are damnably careless in dropping things, and I'm always there to help out. Old habits die hard, I fear, when one comes from Seven Dials.

Time passed as I pondered, strolling along the familiar streets, where my future lay. Uncle Abe was back in work, though the very mention of such a word would induce in him a fit of the staggers and make him as sick as a horse. Aunt Eliza was flourishing now the do-gooders had done their good and gone.

So my contribution to the income of the house was no longer necessary.

The fog had cleared a little by the time I reached Drury Lane, and I paused at the stall of Blind Gerald, the pease-pudding seller, standing like a Roman god, enveloped in steam from his iron pot. There was a young man, wrapped to the eyes against the cold, sucking his way through a dish of peascod, drawing the whole young peas, boiled and buttered, through his teeth, spitting the pods to the gutter.

I joined him, and we ate in silence together, the muffled noises of the metropolis going on around us, but we were like two mariners marooned on an island, with only Blind Gerry's hoarse cry of 'Hot peas. Hot peascod!' to interrupt us. It was very companionable.

'Will you have a small drink with me, sir?' said the young man suddenly, addressing me and handing over a silver flask that had the warm aroma of port and brandy. 'But we have not been introduced.'

'I am Thomas Goane.'

He bowed, and the scarf slipped, revealing a lively, dark face. 'Delighted. And I am Dante Gabriel Rossetti.'

CHAPTER SEVEN

He was, without the shadow of a doubt, one of the most fascinating men that I have ever encountered. I saw much of him for the next year, and found him like a pool in a river. One moment still and silent, dark and contemplative. The next bubbling and sparkling, so that he dazzled you with his shimmering brilliance.

Gabriel Rossetti was only some four or five years older than me, and yet he was so much a man of the world. I had considered myself old for my years, and I think that I was, but Gabriel made me feel a child. There were times when he hurt me by his indifferent cruelty and his thoughtless behaviour. But I knew that he treated all his friends so. And like me they tolerated his waywardness, for they all loved him.

Yet you will be wondering how we came to become so close, merely on the strength of a casual greeting at a peascod seller's stall.

Gabriel was depressed on that night and had taken a stroll for his health, though that sort of fog was little good for the health of man or beast. He was living with Will Huntikins, as he called William Holman Hunt, in a studio rented by Hunt in Cleveland Street. Between Park Crescent and Fitzroy Square.

They were both artists. I had never been greatly interested in painting pictures, though I had splashed a little distemper on walls when the rookery needed decorating. But I had taken to reading the newspapers, and so I had come to know something of life beyond Seven Dials. And I knew a doxy who had mentioned this wild Italian boy, who was always trying to get the whores to pose for him, even though he was perpetually and chronically short of tin.

'You look a good fellow, Tom Goane,' Gabriel had said, as I sipped at his port and brandy in a flask that I later learned he had borrowed from Johnnie Millais, yet another dauber.

I had smiled and nodded, picking a few shreds of pea-pod from between my front teeth. There seemed little comment that one could make. If I agreed it would appear conceited, and if I didn't, then I might lay myself open to a charge of false modesty.

For, in truth, I *did* in honesty consider myself something of a good fellow.

I was struck by the friendly look in those dark eyes, giving away instantly the Italian blood that ran so thick in Gabriel's veins. London folk as a whole do not talk in such a companionable manner to strangers.

'And you have a damnably fine bone structure. Have you ever worked as a model for a painter?'

Because I'm a reasonably handsome fellow, there have been times up around the Haymarket when I've been approached by some of the back-door toffs, wanting me to bugger them and the like. I confess that for a moment I pondered on whether this Rossetti was not one of them.

'You doubt me, Tom?'

'Aye. I do not know what you truly want from me.'

He laughed, throwing back his head and letting the smile burst out. Steam billowed white in the fog as he bellowed his mirth.

'By Hades! You're a dry file, young Goane. Is that what you said your name was? Well, I have a few friends who are always looking for someone who wants to earn a bit of tin — only a bit mind you — by posing for us.'

'Like at Aunt . . . I mean like in the bawdy-houses?'

'Poses plastiques? Heavens! No!! Just so that we can

99

sketch or paint you. We're all so devilish poor, except Johnnie Millais of course, that we all end up drawing each other and that can't go on.'

I had drained the last of his drink, passing it back to him, feeling its insidious warmth ploughing its way through my innards. And I felt something else. A kinship for this young man.

'Right.'

'What?'

'I said "right" and that's what I meant. I am the fellow for you. For some time I have been wondering how to set off and begin to earn my fortune, and what better way than with a bunch of painters.'

'By . . .! Tom, you are one of us. And you must come and meet the rest of the Brotherhood.'

There had been any number of scares of anarchists and radicals in London, and I suddenly cooled and drew back, uncertain. With his small beard and foreign ways, could this Rossetti not be one of them? A mad bomber. An assassin, come to kill and maim. All these thoughts flashed through my mind with the speed of a post-chaise.

'What's wrong, Tom? You look as if you'd stepped in a clump of violets and found they hid a cow-pat.'

I shook my head and the mood passed. 'Nothing, Mister Rossetti.'

'No. I will not have that.'

'What?'

'This "Mister Rossetti" nonsense.'

'But . . .'

'Gabriel, Tom. Call me Gabriel. All my friends do, and I somehow feel that you and I will be friends.'

He reached out and I clasped his hand firmly, feeling him wince and pull back.

'What's wrong, Gabriel?'

'You don't know your own strength, young Tom. You

damned nearly broke the fingers of the most famous unhung artist in England. Nay, in the world.'

'I'm sorry, Gabriel.'

'No. No more of that, my dear fellow. Come, while we are feeling sound in wind and limb, let us repair back to our vaulted chamber in Cleveland Street, and you shall meet the rest of us, if they have found their way through this fog, and if that dormouse Collinson has managed to wake up. Or if he has torn himself away from Christina.'

He stopped as though sinking into a reverie, but I saw his attention had been taken by a shop girl scurrying homewards through the fog. Which had thickened again, and was turning into a throat-grabber.

'What a stunner! Let's follow her, Tom!'

His eyes flamed with eagerness, and his fingers bit into my arm through the sleeve of my coat, but I stood fast on the pavement, resisting his efforts to tug me onto the damp cobbles.

'Damnation! She's gone!'

'We'd never have tracked her down in this, Gabriel. It's worsening.'

'True enough.' His ill temper vanished as fast as it had reared its head, and he was once more himself. 'But what a real stunning stunner!'

She had looked ordinary to me. A pale little slip of a thing, but with coils of hair that burned like a flame. Brighter and more ringletted than Red Carole's even. Hooded eyes, downcast as she'd bustled past us.

Rossetti talked constantly as he walked me back to his rooms through the evening. Though he was sufficiently honest to admit that the rooms weren't actually his but belonged to this other painter, this Will Huntikins, who had paid for them with seventy pounds he'd earned from selling a picture. The idea that one could make that sort of money from simply selling a bit of canvas streaked with colours amazed me, and hardened my resolve to join them.

Thomas Goane has never had much of an eye for art, but he knows what sort of money he likes.

'It's old Sir Sloshua, Tom,' explained Gabriel Rossetti as we hastened towards Cleveland Street and what I hoped might be a warm fire.

'Who?'

'Sloshua? You must have heard of old Sir Sloshua Reynolds, Tom?'

'Sir Joshua Reynolds, do you mean? But is that not a disrespectful manner to talk of someone who is a painter like yourself?'

I thought at first that Rossetti was about to attack me, and my fears of the dangerous gangs returned. Apart from my good two fists, I own that I also carry a small precautionary weapon, after what that officer told me. But not a pistol. Too noisy. And too unreliable. A man can cut your throat and slice you thin while you're still struggling with damp priming.

No, I relied on steel. A slim, leaf-bladed throwing knife, which I wore in a sheath tucked in the back of my trousers where I could easily lay my hand to it.

But he stood off me, and stared at me. Hands on hips like a fishwife ready for trouble.

'Me and Reynolds! You're as mad as M'Naughten, Tom. So you are.' *

'I'm sorry. I can see that I've managed to give offence, and you have my apology.'

* The expression 'As mad as M'Naughten' is a reference to a murder case some years earlier in 1843, when the secretary to Sir Robert Peel had been shot and killed by one Daniel M'Naughten, who was evidently as mad as a hatter. He was found guilty but reprieved when it was put forward that he had no idea, due to insanity, of what he was doing at the time that he killed the secretary. This gave rise to what were known as the 'M'Naughten Rules' which lasted until recent times as the test of criminal responsibility.

His face brightened again. What I could manage to see of it in the fog, that is.

'Say not another word, Tom. You were not to know, but we'll teach you. You see, what we in the PRB believe is that the true art only comes from a detailed observation of things as they really are. And we ...'

'What is the PRB? I have never heard of those initials before.'

'They are ...' here he struck a declamatory pose, throwing back the cape that he wore so that he could lift an arm. 'They are the Pre-Raphaelite Brotherhood, and we shall topple the Royal Academy upon its stupid arse. Come on. Race you to the rooms.'

They were not all there that night, but over the next few days I met them all.

And an odd selection of men they were. Even to my quite inexperienced eye I saw that there were those who would do well and those who would not.

Gabriel Rossetti was their leader, beyond any shadow of a doubt. All the fire and eagerness came from him. But I liked the handsome Johnnie Millais, and from what I saw of his pictures he seemed to me to have the greatest skill with pencil and brush.

Will Hunt was also clearly a real artist, and he and the other two showed their work-in-progress with a mixture of diffidence and pride.

As for the others ... Well, they were all decent fellows, but I could not see any one of them setting the Thames ablaze with their art. There was Tom Woolner, who I first attempted to befriend but found him distant with me. He sculpted, and was the most bitter of them all against the Academy. He called it a 'collection of old men engaged in plunging knives into the living breast of modern sculpture'.

I met Gabriel's brother William that first evening, and

103

liked him, though he was no painter. Nor was the fellow that I liked most at a first meeting. The limping Frederick Stephens, who also seemed glad to welcome a newcomer to their group.

The last of the seven was the dormouse. James Collinson, who had been a student at the Academy and who lived up to his nickname by falling into a deep sleep on every occasion that I saw him.

And there was I, young Tom Goane, among such rebel firebrands. Knowing nothing of art, and caring a great deal less.

I sat in the chilly, high-ceilinged room in Cleveland Street that bitter night and heard them as they argued and wrangled over whether Keats was greater than Shelley and King Alfred of higher stature than Chaucer.

For me they might have argued as to whether the Devonport Slogger would beat Black Pompey at the 'Friars in a week's time.*

Gabriel had introduced me with 'This brave young fellow and I battled our way through the pea-souper against the forces of evil and oppression. His name is Thomas Goane, and he has great expectations from a mysterious stranger in a black cloak. But for the present he is here. Naught else concerns us.'

And I will say this for those young men, that nothing else did concern them. I spent many months with them, and at no time did any of them query my being there. I posed for them when called on and helped out around their studios. They were times of no great significance and I did not consider them important.

Yet when I look back retrospectively on them, I see that those months through the spring and summer of 1849 and onwards well into 1850 were quite vital to me. For during them I turned away from Seven Dials, though I could never

* He did, by knocking him out in the forty-ninth round.

ever throw it off completely. And I set Uncle Abe and Aunt Eliza a little apart from me. Realising their worth but also, like the fledgling leaving the nest, seeing that there was a time to come and a time to go.

They were not short of a penny or two, and I was one mouth less for them to feed. The money still came in from my benefactor and I allowed them to keep it. I truly do not know whether the man in the cloak knew where I was during this time, and for many of those months I did not care. But from what I suspected of Aunt Eliza, I would surmise that he was not ignorant of my whereabouts.

EDITORIAL NOTE: *There have been many excellent volumes covering all aspects of the life and times of the Pre-Raphaelite Brotherhood and their works can be seen in any of the great museums and art galleries of England. The next book and a half of the Journals of Thomas Goane are packed with the trivia of those days. But they are hardly of importance to the general reader and I have taken the liberty of editing them down to a couple of chapters, covering incidents that are clearly of greater moment in the development of young Tom.*

The first is set in the summer of 1849 and, I am sad to say, is yet another example of Tom's unhealthy interest in the opposite sex.

Both Will Hunt and Johnnie Millais had shown pictures in the Academy that year. And both had sold them, though poor Will endured a purgatorial wait until the tin arrived for his painting.

Johnnie's was called *Isabella* and showed a group of men and women seated round a table, one of them at the front kicking a dog. I was plagued with illness that summer, and spent too long on my back in the rookery, missing the cheerful company of Gabriel and the others.

105

I am sure that they would have used me for one of the models, as they were perpetually short of tin to pay a professional model. There is nobody in that painting that I did not know. But it may be of interest that a part of Tom Goane *is* there, frozen in oils, for ever and a day. Johnnie was not happy with the leg of the rogue kicking at the hound, and I was around one hot day, with my trousers rolled up above my knee, and he sketched my leg, saying that it could well have filled a pair of tights to perfection. And there is my finely turned calf for all to see.

Will Hunt sent in a picture with a title that I noted down at the time in my books, for I could surely never have remembered it. Indeed it was a bigger name than the whole picture: *Rienzi Vowing to Obtain Justice for the Death of His Young Brother, Slain in a Skirmish between the Colonna and the Orsini Factions.*

Phew!

By the time I was feeling more bobbish and up and about once more, I found that Hunt and Rossetti had been given the noble order of the boot from their landlord. Will was scavenging for rooms and Gabriel had returned to the bosom of his family in Charlotte Street.

So I resumed living in Seven Dials, but moved around a deal with the others. Though I was several years younger than the youngest of them, it made little difference, and they accepted me in their talks and their jokes. On certain days, I wondered why. And I think now that there was something in them all that made them want to change and improve. Not only the world of art, but people. And not just me.

Hunt had his Annie Miller and Rossetti his Lizzie Siddal. One a slut of a child, younger than me, from a poor, poor neighbourhood. The other a shop assistant from a place selling bonnets.

Both of them absolute stunners.

And who did I have?

I came across Gabriel one afternoon, when I was on the way towards recovery, and he and Hunt were also on the move. To a studio they'd borrowed, where they both intended to do some sketches from life. They were in high spirits as they'd begged and borrowed enough cash to pay for a professional model, and they hoped to garnish enough from a session of three hours with her to utilise in several drawings.

'Tommikins!' shouted Gabriel as soon as he saw me. 'Good meeting indeed. Ouch!'

The 'ouch' was accompanied by his hands flying to his face and his then falling to his knees, where he rolled around, coat-tails dragging in the dust, bellowing like a stallion at the gelding.

When I say that this performance took place in the middle of Oxford Street a little after midday, with the pavements thronged with shoppers and clerks at their luncheon, you will begin to have the merest inkling of what a trial and tribulation Dante Gabriel Rossetti could be to his friends.

I rushed to his aid, but Will Hunt held out a warning hand. 'He is like the old man of the sea in the tales of Sinbad. Aid him now and you will be for ever in his thrall.'

'But what is amiss with him? It appears that he has suffered some kind of brain seizure.'

Hunt laughed, his black beard thrust up towards the blue summer sky. 'Perdition! If that were all!'

'Lockjaw! A mad dog has bitten him?' I was partly jesting, in the mocking manner that they all used towards each other.

'Tom! Maniac!' That was the name that Rossetti used towards Will Huntikins. 'I am dying, Egypt. Dying.'

There was already a considerable crowd ringing us, among which I saw Dipping Roger, up to his own tricks. Which I decided was no concern of mine.

'What of, Rossetti?' said I.

'What?'

'What are you dying of?'

'Bloody toothache, Tom. Toothache!'

And that was all. For all his bravado, Gabriel was a fearful coward. In the words of Aunt Eliza, he was the sort of person who is all wind and piss. Or if it were a woman, she would be described as all mouth and no drawers.

And it was not only fear of pain that preoccupied Rossetti. There was another thing.

'And another thing, Tom. Blast it, man, keep your eyes off her jugs! Can you stand a little closer? That's it. Much better.'

I was there, clad in a small hand towel, which covered only the barest of my essentials, pressed up against Scotch Helen. Their professional model. Over the years I had seen Scotch Helen in many places, and in none of them had she looked as though she had been earning her money by modelling.

But times changed.

'I 'ad to give it up when I 'ad the bairns,' she explained to me while Hunt and Rossetti were adjusting the blinds, endeavouring to get the lighting right for the pose. I was a warrior king and Helen was my helpless slave, kneeling at my feet and begging me for mercy.

I rather liked the idea.

'Can you put your hands around his legs, there's a good girl?' said Hunt.

'I'm no 'is good girl,' whispered Helen, doing as she was told, taking the opportunity to reach up under the towel and give the jewel casket a quick once over.

Although I glowed a healthy and embarrassed red at it, I admit that I rather hoped that the once-over might become a twice-over.

Helen was a damnably pretty piece of whore's meat, being

taller than the average and with the most stunning black hair, framing a pale face with lively eyes. She was not over-large around the bosom, but they had a fine, perky look to them. A sort of 'damn your eyes!' insolence that I found arousing.

'Watch it, Tommy,' she hisses to me, while the two artists are locked in argument about how tired this warrior king ought to be. 'Keep your weather eye on your flag-pole. It's on its way up past half-mast.'

At first I wondered what she meant, then I broke my stiff pose and found that it was not only the pose that had become stiff. John Thomas was attempting to lift his colours, climbing higher than a Newgate neck-tie. To check the movement, I reached down and adjusted the towel.

'Keep bloody still, Tom! This is hard enough as it is with Maniac saying you ought to be more exhausted.'

'Wish they'd go away, Tommy,' whispers the lady. 'I'd show them a bit of exhaustion. Both have to lie down we would! How about it?'

'Sssh,' I said, feeling events rising out of my control and trying not to let it show. Which was a forlorn hope.

And to place a cap on it all, Helen begins to sing, very quiet, a ditty popular at some of the more rowdy places of entertainment.

It had a chorus that went something like this:

> 'We went walking, walking in the park,
> And I asked her if she's willing for a lark,
> She says "Yes, yes, yes, but only if it's dark."
> So, I knows that I'm in luck, luck, luck,
> And I'm glad that I'm a drake and not a duck,
> She says ',Yes, yes, yes, I'm ready for a . . ."
> Boom tarara, boom tarara, boom boom boom.'

It loses a lot from not being done with the actions.

And as Rossetti and Hunt seemed near to coming to

blows, Scotch Helen is not averse to showing me one or two of those actions.

Though only fifteen at this time, I was well built for my age. I felt it necessary to remind you, gentle readers, of that fact, less you imagine that I was still like some down-cheeked schoolboy.

'It is no good, Gabriel. I will not have it so. He will have marched and fought for a good hour and he will be . . . wilting. Look at Tom! He's standing there with that trollop looking like a Grenadier on parade in Hyde Park.'

'Marching for an hour, and still fresh and ready for action,' replies Rossetti. 'And Tom there is looking damnably as if he's about to present his firing-piece for action.'

I blushed a yet deeper red.

'And I say a man cannot march hard for an hour without he looks fatigued.'

'And I say he can.'

'Cannot!'

'Can!'

'I feel a wee bit hungry, Tom. You've no got anything I could nibble on?'

It was an insidious whisper, barely audible to me, but quite beyond the hearing of the angry artists.

Rossetti and Hunt had moved over to the window and were peering out across the streets. Far below them I could faintly hear a rhubarb seller shouting his wares. Helen's head was resting near my knee, and her tongue flicked out like a landlord's warrant and touched my bare flesh, making me jump in the air.

Then her head was resting against my thigh.

Then her head was resting . . . higher.

'I say that he could not!'

'Hellfire and damnation, Maniac! Tom is a soldier and a great leader. He could keep it up as long as the sun shone. And there's an end to it.'

'You're a bonny laddie, Tom Goane,' hisses Helen again, sitting in such a way that my craft is only a scant inch from her ivory harbour. 'You'd be the answer to a maiden's prayer if what yon coves say is true. Aboot you keepin' it up as long as the sun shines.'

'Shut up! Just shut your mouth, Helen,' says I, wishing that the earth would open and swallow me.

It is not the earth that swallows me.

'Does that shut my mouth all right?' she asked me, mumbling somewhat:

'Don't talk with your mouth full,' I tell her, feeling that's one up to me. By now I am near the stage of being past caring. But Rossetti and Hunt are still arguing, their backs fortunately turned to me.

But if they should turn round! I reached down and squeezed the young bobtail by the apple dumplings. Not too hard, but hard enough to make her cease her games for the moment.

'You backgammon bugger!' she says, loud enough for my friends to nearly hear her. 'You're lucky I didn't just bite down on your bullet.'

But she smiles while she says it.

'Very well!'

'Very well, Gabriel.'

They spin about on their heels and stalk across the dusty, paint-splattered floor of the studio towards us. Side by side like two pickled herrings on a plate. Helen slides submissively lower, though I can feel her shaking with a fit of sniggering.

'Tom.'

'Tom.'

'Let me,' says Rossetti.

'Let me,' says Will Huntikins.

'All right,' says Rossetti.

'Very well,' says Hunt, and they both stand there looking

quizzically at each other, now more like barn owls than pickled herrings.

'Gabriel,' I said to him, 'you tell me what you and Will have decided.'

He smiled, eyes widening with delight as the merits of his idea aroused his enthusiasm.

'Will and I are not in agreement as to whether it is possible for a man to march at a fixed pace for one hour and not feel unduly fatigued. So we have elected to put that to the test. We will leave this studio in . . .' he paused to consult a silver half-hunter. His father's again, I fear. 'In three minutes. And we will proceed at a firm speed for one hour. Can you and the girl find something to do for that time?'

He might as well asked if the sun wouldn't mind rising in the east and setting in the west. I assumed a serious visage and nodded.

'I believe we might somehow struggle along in your absence, Gabriel.'

Neither of them noticed the note of mockery in my voice, so taken up they were with their own argument. For a Pre-Raphaelite must have every detail correct.

'Ready, Will?'

'Ready, Signor Rossetti. Let us to battle.'

And off they went, those two most marvellous men, stamping their feet like sentries on picket duty, off through the door, which Rossetti shut smartly behind them, and we kept our poses as the feet drummed away down the stairs. Down and down and down.

'Let's go see them along the way,' said Helen, jumping up and padding barefoot to the window, her bottom rolling like two ferrets trapped in a cotton sack.

Still clutching the towel to me, for the Lord knows what reason as we were quite alone, I joined her, easing aside a corner of the blind and fixing my eye to the casement, watching for Hunt and Gabriel to appear.

Which they finally did, striding along, Gabriel twirling his cane, neither speaking nor even looking to each other, heads rigidly ahead. Brushing aside other users of the footpath as if they had no substance. Finally disappearing around the next corner in the general direction of the Regent's Canal.

Which left just Scotch Helen and myself.

'Well,' she said.

'Well?' I replied, letting the corner of the blind fall back into place, so that the only bright light in the studio was aimed at the podium where only a few moments earlier we had been warrior king and captive slave.

'That looks like a comfortable place to rest your arse on, over there,' she said, pointing with her long leg towards a pile of old blankets scattered in a corner of the room, in the angle alongside the wall.

'Then let's go and rest, as we have some fifty-seven minutes before those two warriors return from their route march.'

'It will not be a long engagement, then?'

'But fierce,' I replied, picking her up and carrying her across the room, planting a large kiss on each fire-tipped cone.

As things came to pass, there were three furious sorties which finally resulted in both armies being damnably fatigued on the return of Rossetti and Hunt. Both of them were panting and streaming sweat as they staggered in and no more painting was done that day. And I was grateful for it, as I doubt that any part of me could have stood erect after Scotch Helen.

In my heart I thanked Gabriel and Will for that foolish yet timely march. As I have heard said: if they be mad, then I wish all men were mad.

CHAPTER EIGHT

The plan among them was to present three paintings at the coming Exhibition of 1850, each signed with the initials of the PRB, and so bring themselves to the forefront of the artistic world.

Like so many of their plans, it was Gabriel who placed the kitten among the terriers, by showing his picture earlier and in another place.

But that was still to come, and the group were still to some degree united. Though we were all damnably tired of Woolner, who was working in the summer heat on a great statue of some ten feet in height. In clay. And it must needs be kept damp. This involved us, and mainly poor gimpy Stephens and myself, in constantly climbing a step-ladder and pouring endless pots of water on the wretched thing. I was not sad to see less of the cynical Woolner.

And it was towards the beginning of that year that I met one of the great men of my time. And the great man's wife.

John Ruskin was someone who I had heard of even before meeting Gabriel and falling headlong into the turbulent waters of the world of pictures and art. He was a writer and painter himself, of outstanding distinction, whose word was law in matters of Art, with a capital 'A' to show its importance.

Luckily enough for the PRB, they had the might of Ruskin behind them. Without it they might have foundered at the first hint of rough seas and stormy criticism.

He had supported them in correspondence and in the learned journals. And he had come to befriend them. Particularly did he become close to young Johnnie Millais.

When first I met Ruskin, I was struck forcibly by one main characteristic.

He was a very *silly* man.

Lacking any kind of awareness of what went on in the world. And yet he was older than any of the Brotherhood. He was thirty, and near as a toucher old enough to be my father. He held his head very upright and always sported formal clothes, contrasting oddly with the informality of the other, younger artists. Particularly it was odd and somewhat amusing to see him locked in conversation with the shorter, excitable, flamboyant Rossetti or the striking and immaculately fashionable Millais.

But Ruskin was married.

And there was the rub.

EDITORIAL NOTE: *The bare bones of one of the greatest scandals of Victorian England are simple, and we are fortunate in having Tom Goane's Journals to convey a little of the flavour of the very beginning of the affair. The marriage of the Ruskins was at best formal, and at worst . . . it is kinder for me as a scholar to draw a veil over it at worst. But his wife was to leave him in a sensational divorce case and marry Millais. There were elements of society that never forgave either of them. Ruskin declined over the years and ended his life in a fog of madness. Among the most bitter opponents of the divorce was Queen Victoria herself. The reader can obtain some idea of how strong such disapproval can be by the dying words of Millais, so many years on, when his last thoughts were of the matter. He said, 'Beg the Queen that she will* at last *receive my wife.' This was* forty-one *years after his marriage.*

It was all because of Hunt that I was to meet John Ruskin and his young wife.

Will was busily engaged in bringing another of his length-

115

ily titled visions to fruition ready for the next Exhibition at the Academy. This was to be at the beginning of May in 1850. His new work was called *A Converted British Family Sheltering a Christian Missionary from the Persecution of the Druids*. Why he could not slosh on some paint and call it 'Hope' or 'Faith' or even 'Charity' was quite beyond me.

It was a crowd of mainly half-clad natives, all of quite amazing beauty, lurking around in a bothy by some water, while a panting priest, who has the look to me of a Papist, sits and fans himself like a dowager with the vapours. Outside the hut are a crowd of other revolting peasants hallooing their way after another poor prelate who is clearly about to be nabbed by the bristles and well dunked.

And if he's a Papist, then it serves him right.

At this time the old Pope had the damned nerve to tell his red-cap Newman to split the whole of the country up between his Latin-eaters. *Our* country, mind you. I wasn't the only one who felt exercised by it, I can tell you. Uncle Abe was as good a Protestant as the next man when it came to the Romanists and organised protests in the rookeries, burning effigies of the Pope.

You may be wondering what part Tom Goane played in this painting. I was one of those peasants in the hut. That is me you can see, if the painting still exists, on the left-hand side, with my back turned.*

It was one of the hardest jobs that I ever landed myself with, and as it was for a friend there was very little soskins in it for me. Still, I liked Will, and Uncle Abe and Aunt Eliza were well provided for by the man in the cloak.

I had been posing with a street urchin whom Hunt had found to be one of the other peasants, and who had the face

* This very picture does indeed still exist, and I have seen it. It is hung in the Ashmolean Museum in Oxford, and is exactly as Tom describes it. He is the boy on the left, standing on tip-toe with a knife at his belt.

of a fallen cherub and the manners of a gutter-tom. He drove Hunt to the brink of blind rage by his habit of never asking when he wished to be relieved. Thus necessitating much work with a mop and bucket.

'Only another ten minutes and then we'll break and go round to Johnnie's for a bite. Ruskin's coming round with Effie.'

'Effie?'

'Ruskin's wife. Euphemia. What Gabriel calls a real stunner. And I've seen some stunners in my day. Makes Annie look what she is, poor little girl. Effie Ruskin is a lady, and woe betide any man who treats her in any other manner.'

'Is she as old as Mister Ruskin?'

'Don't move your hand, you damnable spawn of Satan! Sorry, Tom, I didn't catch that.'

'Effie. Is she as old as Mister Ruskin?'

'Bless me, no. Nobody is as old as John Ruskin. He's a good-hearted fellow, and we know what a debt we owe him. But I truly doubt if he has a young bone in his body or a light thought in his head. Ruskin was born fully clothed at age thirty, with a book in his hand and already jawing fit to burst.'

'How old is his wife?'

Hunt paused in his daubing, a brush filled with light brown paint dripping in his hand, dribbling on the floor of the studio. 'Must be . . . let me see. They married in April of '48. She was just twenty then. She must be twenty-one going on towards twenty-two now.'

'Pretty? Truly?'

The PRB had the habit of applying the name of a 'stunner' rather freely, and I wondered how deserved it was.

'Damnably. Millais says that when she smiles he's sure he can hear the fluttering of celestial wings. Yes. Pretty and proud.'

Those last ten minutes in the modelling day stretched into all eternity. I had to stand in the least natural position known to man, on the corner of a rug on which Hunt had spilled a few dried leaves. Not to mention what the urchin had also spilled on it. Up on my toes, with my hands in a sort of praying way. Sadly, my head was turned right away from Will Hunt, and you will not see my face, more's the pity. But you will see what a fine set-up chap I was for fifteen.

Apart from a pair of short flannel drawers, I was unclad. My fate in most of my modelling assignments. A quiver of arrows was slung on my left hip, in an inconvenient place if I had been holding a bow as well. But I was not, Hunt being unable to lay his hands on one in time.

A dagger at my right hip and a cracked hunting horn completed my outfit. I was eternally grateful that it was not winter, as I'm sure that the wasting sickness would have whisked me away with it.

After such a tiring day, the thought of a meal with Millais was a relief. Rossetti was also to be there with his quiet and too-clever (I thought) sister, Christina.

And the Ruskins.

Millais sat himself at the head of the carved oak table at his home, as was his right as host. Ruskin as the honoured guest sat at his right, with Rossetti next to him. Christina was at the bottom of the table, where she sat and sulked the entire evening because her brother would not compliment her on a sonnet she had read out before the meal.

For myself I thought it a poor mooning thing, with no reality to it and a deal of lovesick swainery.

And I sat next to Mrs Euphemia Ruskin.

Hunt was right. She was a stunning beauty, though she appeared to be lost for too much of the evening in some solitary private grief. Her hair was dark, and tugged back

118

and tied with a ribbon of green silk, shot through with a light blue. Her dress was simple, sweeping out in a wide skirt. Its colour was a light blue, matching the shade in the hair ribbon.

We were introduced before the meal, but Hunt had dallied over-long with his revolting peasants, and there was no time for small-talk. I was pleased to find myself sitting next to her, as I knew that the others would immediately lock themselves into a private conclave on art. The storm-clouds around Christina's brow indicated that she would be poor company. Thus, Euphemia and I were more or less thrown together by fate.

I observed a most singular fact about Mr and Mrs Ruskin. At no time before or during the meal did they actually look at each other. Nor did they speak, unless some turn of the general conversation rendered it necessary. As I was in the company of my elders, and some might say betters, I followed my usual practice of holding my tongue. But Mrs Ruskin would not allow this, pressing me for details of my life and prattling on in an undertone about herself and about her husband.

She made it most transparent that she admired him, and to be sure she was not in error, for there was much in his intellect to admire. And yet there was something amiss, and I could not for a moment place my finger upon it.

And yet she gave me clues enough. One in particular I recall well, for the general embarrassment that it appeared to cause everyone there.

Everyone, that is, except for John Ruskin himself.

He had been talking eagerly of his hopes to travel abroad, where he wished to see as much as possible of the works of the great European masters with whom he was not yet familiar.

'It is my express desire,' he said, his voice dominating the table, beating us into a submissive silence. 'It is my express desire to immerse myself in their rich aura of divine sensuality.'

'I am delighted to hear that this is your wish, John,' says Euphemia, as chilling as a St James's ice cart in July. 'Perhaps some of that enthusiasm may escape into other spheres of your life.'

There was a great silence, as though someone had let slip a cheesy thumper in front of the Queen. And I deduced that all there except myself knew the undercurrent that dragged the evening down.

And it was a great shame, for the food was quite excellent, being simple fare but well cooked. As I know that the gentler readers will be interested in it, I have copied out what we ate there.

We began with a soup. A purée of artichokes, followed by slices of sole, grilled with an oyster sauce. Then a large bowl of whitebait. To which I was becoming uncommon partial.

There was a saddle of mutton, which was universal at such affairs, and a roasted turkey with a fruit sauce, which Millais claimed a friend from the Americas had suggested.

It was not well received.

Sweetbreads in a rich celery sauce and vegetables. Cabbage and parsnips. I confess that I have never enjoyed cabbage since being served it as a small child. Another infant at the table assured me that it was not grown but drawn from the nostrils of drowned seamen, and I believed him. Absurd though the fancy is, I can never look cabbage in the eye without a cold shudder.

And, of course, three dishes of boiled potatoes, larded with butter and sprinkled with parsley.

With a discussion on the classical influences on seventeenth-century architecture, led by Ruskin—and followed by Ruskin as well—we had a brace of ducks and pheasants.

The usual puddings and jellies.

The wine flowed, as it always did at any meeting or meal

where the Pre-Raphaelite Brotherhood were foregathered. And still Ruskin talked.

And talked.

And talked.

I have not the least doubt that much of what he said was of great moment, and had I tried to understand it I would be a better and wiser man today. But it was all far above my head, like a great colourful balloon that floated over while I stood among the flowers and gaped up at it.

You may be imagining to yourselves that it was a damnably dull evening for Tom Goane.

Not so.

For it was not too large a table, and I found that my chair had been set too close to that of Mrs Ruskin. Simple politeness forbade that I should attempt to draw myself away, but I found the warmth and pressure of her leg against mine a constant distraction from John Ruskin's learned discourse to us.

And things did not improve. Like a young whore I knew who ended up writing poems. She went from bed to verse. So things went from bad to worse.

We wore napkins on our laps, and I found that mine had that habit of always slipping off to the carpet. And that night was no exception. Smack in the middle of my second helping of the mutton. I reached down to pick it up, and discovered that Euphemia had done the same thing at the same time. Our hands brushed below the table, and I felt her fingers feather against mine. And squeeze.

It was all so quick that I might have been mistaken.

Yet I knew that I was not.

And during the slicing of the ducks, which fell by chance to me, I was somewhat nervous, having the eyes of such an august company on me, and I let the knife slip from my greasy fingers. Once again, as I stooped to pick it up, I found that Effie was there before me. Handing me the knife, with a muttered word. And I in turn, suddenly made to feel like a conspirator, muttered my thanks.

But worse was to come.

During the eating of the desserts, Christina had risen from the table, saying that she felt unwell. But Ruskin scarcely noticed her absence, and Hunt, Millais and Rossetti still hung on every word of their idol. Which left Effie and me to our own devices.

At first I imagined that I had dropped something on my lap, when I felt a weight on my napkin. Light as a chicken bone. And my left hand went down to remove it, my right hand being occupied in transferring a largish portion of apple jelly from my plate to my mouth.

My oath! It was no chicken bone. It was the tips of a lady's fingers, and I think I break no confidences when I tell you that the fingers belonged to Mrs Ruskin.

I near vomited in my shock. Her married scarcely a year and a half, and with her husband not more than a yard away from her. I fear my face betrayed my shock, and I fear also that I started.

Gabriel and Johnnie both looked at me, though Hunt was lost in listening to Ruskin's discourse. Gabriel was damned quick to pick up what was going on, and he spotted that her right hand and my left were both out of sight. And he winked at me, turning back immediately to listen to the master with an exaggerated expression of interest that would have made me laugh at any other time.

Johnnie Millais, like that little lady in the shrubbery of Buckingham Palace, was not amused.

He had peculiarly narrow eyes, set in that handsome face, and they flashed fire at me. I knew that he was the leader of Ruskin's disciples, and I saw that this must be why I had angered him. To try to turn his anger, I snatched my hand away from Effie, feeling my face turn crimson as I did so.

'You are too warm, Mister Goane?' Suddenly Ruskin,

after ignoring me for the best part of two hours, chose that moment to look at me and bring me into the conversation.

'No. Yes. That is, I am not sure, sir.'

It was a deuced awkward moment, and was saved for me by Hunt, though I think he did it accidentally. 'What an awful splash of paint on your coat, Tom. The colour of horse manure, isn't it?'

I started at that, and looked him in the eye. 'Why, so it is, Will,' I replied. 'And it exactly matches the shade of your cravat.'

There was a loud burst of laughter at that, led by Rossetti, and applause at Will's discomfiture. It took several minutes of explanation before Ruskin could be made to understand the point of the jest, but he then laughed as heartily as any of us.

The moment had passed.

Effie had imbibed more than a lady should at such a dinner party and was becoming restive again, rubbing the side of her foot against my leg. Letting it rise higher and higher, and pressing her thigh against me. Which made it hard to hear all about Ruskin's trials and tribulations with his new easel that he had recently purchased.

'I must have a little fresh air. It is quite stifling in here. Mister Goane, will you do me the honour of accompanying me and we may leave these other gentlemen to set the art world to rights?'

Euphemia had scooped the pool. There was no way at all that I could, as a gentleman, refuse her request. Millais looked daggers at me. Rossetti grinned, like the cheeky monkey that he was. Hunt scarcely noticed what had been said, and Ruskin smiled a saintly, benevolent smile. Rather like a successful poisoner seeing off one of his victims. Or so it appeared to my poor fevered imagination.

'Yes, I would be delighted. Unless . . .' a hope sprang to

my mind, 'Unless your husband would prefer to accompany you on a . . .'

'No. Not at all, my dear young friend. My wife enjoys the company of younger men. Have a good time. Now, as I was saying, the easel is not built to really . . .'

Did I imagine it, or was Rossetti smothering a muffled laugh behind his wipe?

But I didn't wait to find out, feeling Effie's hand hook on my arm, leading me through the big French windows and out into the cool London air. Closing the windows behind us.

'There. I truly did believe that I would stifle.'

Out in the garden the first scents of spring were wafting about among the bushes. I stole a glance over my shoulder, seeing the yellow glow of the lamps in the dining-room. I could just see Johnnie Millais's back, and even as I watched he too turned casually around in his seat and peered out of the window in our direction.

'Are those wallflowers?' asked Effie, steering me further from the house, towards a part of the garden where the trees foregathered and hung overhead, making a shaded arbour of it.

'I . . . I believe so.' My damned voice cracked and creaked its way around the words I wanted.

No more words were exchanged until we were within the secluded clearing, when Effie—Mrs Ruskin—stopped and looked up at me. I was aware that the air seemed suddenly very still, and the world was hushed, as though waiting for what she had to say.

'Tom?'

'Yes.'

'Ooooooh! Boo hoo!'

I have always felt that 'boo hoo' does not properly convey the noise of anyone weeping, but it will have to serve.

Euphemia collapsed in my arms in great floods of tears,

and I was hard put not to drop her, so unexpected was the event. But I managed to help her to a small rustic bench at the side of the clearing and I contrived to wipe away her tears and calm her somewhat.

This involved me in holding her close, and patting her on the back and here and there to relieve her sadness.

She made little move to the patting on the back, but the 'here and there' brought her close to a boiling point of emotion. The tears gradually ceased, but she refused to let me release her, and she in turn was allowing her ten pink soldiers to go a'wandering about my person in a manner that would have been indelicate in a Hoxton trull and was positively bewildering in a respectable married lady.

'Come, Effie, do try and compose yourself. And pray tell me what is amiss with you? Whatever it is, it cannot be as severe as all that.'

'Oh, you are too kind, Tom. Too kind to a wretch like me. And you cannot know the half of what lies between my husband and myself.'

'Is he cruel?'

'No. No, John is the kindest of mortals. If only he were to beat me. To take a riding crop and flog me with it until the blood flowed from my wounds and bathed the grass at my feet.'

Which I personally thought was laying it on a little strong.

'Then what? I fear that I cannot comprehend how too much kindness can so sadden you.'

She was much quieter, for which I was grateful. But she still gripped my hands tightly in hers, and kept them pressed to her bosom, which rose and fell in a manner that I found more than somewhat distracting.

'You know, do you not Tom?'

'What?'

'What should . . . but perhaps you are too young to know.

125

Yes, I am sure you are and I am wrong to try and draw you into my worries.'

'I may be lacking in years, but I think that I am yet wise in the ways of the world, Effie,' I said grandly, drawing myself up and wondering if my sprouting chin showed to good effect in the pale moonlight.

'Very well. You know then, perhaps, what should happen between a man and his wife?'

Had she begun to babble to me in some outlandish nigger tongue I could not have been more confused. What could she mean? Unless . . . she could not mean that?

Yes, reader, she meant precisely *that*!

'You mean . . . ?'

'Yes. What should take place when they are alone together in the privacy of their bedroom.'

'I . . . have heard. Dash it! Yes, I do know, Effie. But how does this . . .'

'We do not.'

'Not?'

'Not.'

'Not ever?'

'No, Tom. John and I have never once been united in the way that a man and woman should. He has never tried to . . . never once.'

My experiences at Aunt Eliza's had brought me into contact with most kinds of oddities. Floggers and flogged. Corset and boot boys. Hussingtons, who were old fellows unable to do more than fumble or watch. Back-garden rogers. All kinds. And some of them who were, for some reason or other, unable to perform what they wanted.

But I had never heard of anyone who didn't want to perform anything at all! Especially with a handsome filly like Euphemia as wife. She'd have brought a cold kettle to the boil in no time at all.

'But what can be wrong?'

She began to blubber a little, then made an effort to pull herself together, breaking away from me and standing a few paces in front of me. 'John says that he has seen many pictures of women ... unclad women ... and that ... that I am not made as they are. That I am different. Deformed.'

I thought that she was about to break down again, and tried to divert her by asking her to tell me more.

'He is not ready to ... cannot ... because of the way that I am made. He tells me that I repulse him.'

To my horror, Effie began to struggle and writhe about like a dusky dancer, finally lifting up her dress and heaving up layers of petticoats, until I could see the white flash of her gams in the moonlight.

'Come here and aid me, Tom. Pull down my drawers and tell me what you see.'

I swear that I have never been so amazed in all of my life. It was all some sort of dream. Or could it be a nightmare?

'Quickly!'

Her voice was raised and I felt a horror that Ruskin and the others would hear her and come running out, finding me in the most compromising position since Adam was caught with a mouthful of rosy pippin.

There was only one thing that I could do and, manfully, I did it.

Dropped to my knees in front of her, and reached up under her lifted skirt, plucking at the drawstring of her drawers, easing them down until they were a few inches above knee-level. The still evening was filled with the musky perfume of her body, rousing Sir John Thomas to fearful heights of passion, making my trousers uncomfortably tight around the jewel box.

'There. Now what do you see?'

It was simply what I had expected to see on any normal woman. In the same place, and seemingly of the same size. After what she had told me of Ruskin's revulsion, I had half-closed my eyes, expecting Heaven knows what horrors. Some swollen monstrosities or some raddling disease.

'I see, though it is hard to make out in this moonlight, what I have always seen in the past in such a place.'

Could I truly be having this conversation with a married lady after a dinner party?

'Then look closer. Come . . .' And she dragged me by the hair letting her skirts fall a little, pulling me in so close that I could not only see but also taste. 'Is that what other women have? I am made the way that other women are made?'

'Yes,' said I, unable to resist the temptation to explore a little, which produced a wriggle and something like a smothered laugh from Effie.

'You are sure?'

'I am sure. Effie, you are made in every feature like any other woman that I have ever known.'

'And you have known many?'

Honesty battled with pride.

Pride won.

'Hundreds. And all much like you, but few as stunning in that way.'

I thought for a moment that I heard footsteps and hastily tugged myself clear, rising panting to my feet again. Euphemia in turn reached under her dress and adjusted her drawers, letting her skirts fall back so that a certain propriety was established again between us.

'He says that I am ugly, and that the women in the paintings of the great classical masters are not like me. That they are not flawed but are perfect. That there is . . . no hair . . . down there. And that they look sweet and clean. He says . . .' again the sob in her voice. 'He says that he cannot imagine that such women would . . . would *smell*.'

'Of course you smell, Effie. But it is the sweetest scent that ever I knew and one that brings naught but pleasure to a man's nostrils. And in all other ways you are nothing short of perfect.'

In a voice that might raise the dead, Effie Ruskin threw back her head and called out in her distress, 'Then why in the name of God can John not get it up?'

At that moment John Ruskin materialised from behind a large elm tree, his voice as controlled and urbane as ever. 'What is my wife talking about, Mister Goane? What can I not get up?'

CHAPTER NINE

'What is my wife talking about, Mister Goane? What can I not get up?'

Had I been struck on the head by a hundredweight of horse dung I do not think that the shock could possibly have been any greater. Ruskin had materialised from the earth, like the demon king in a children's show. My first thought, *after* I had ensured that my breeches were unfouled, was to wonder how much of our conversation he had overheard. Then my common sense came a little to my aid and I perceived that if he had heard any more than that last cry, he would not be standing there looking politely interested. Not even a man like Ruskin would have been so in control.

All this flashed through my mind in less time than it takes to dot an 'i' and I was once more myself as I turned to face him, seeing for the first time that the other three were with him. Rossetti grinning broadly at what he clearly saw as my come-uppance. Hunt puzzled. And Millais staring at me and at Effie as though the fires of all the forges blazed in his eyes.

'What can you not get up?' I repeated rather foolishly, as though it had been a child's conundrum.

'Yes.'

Effie stood at my elbow, where I could just see her from the outer range of my vision. It might have been the silvering effect of the moon, but her face looked as pale as death.

'Your easel.' I pattered a silent prayer to my gods for the thought.

'My easel?' Ruskin was still simply politely bewildered. Not in any manner exercised by what was happening, though it seemed to me a world of absurdities.

'Yes. Your wife, Mrs Ruskin,' in case he'd forgotten who she was, 'Mrs Ruskin was telling me all about your new easel. The one that you were discussing so entertainingly over the meal.'

'What of it?'

It was a blind shot in the dark that nonetheless succeeded in striking the gold.

'Mrs Ruskin was merely amplifying what you had said and was explaining that you had a great deal of difficulty in erecting it.'

'What? Erecting it?'

'Yes. That was the moment at which you joined us, when she was saying that you were unable to get it up.'

Rossetti leaned against a tree, seemingly overwhelmed by a violent coughing fit, while Hunt continued to look puzzled. Johnnie Millais spun on his heel and stalked back towards the house.

'I see. Of course. And I may say that Euphemia is quite correct.' He took me by the arm, quite ignoring poor Effie, who was clearly on the edge of a total collapse. And led me back again indoors. Keeping up a flood of boring information about his damned easel, until I almost wondered if it might not have been easier to have told him the truth and taken the consequences.

'There is a locking nut at the side which stubbornly rejects all my best endeavours. Without the correct functioning of this nut, the whole easel is unstable and has an alarming tendency to slip and topple.'

I did my best to contribute with a little murmur here and there and much nodding of my head.

'Thus, Euphemia is accurate in what she was telling you. By the way, where is she?'

'I believe that Gabriel and Will are assisting her in. She was finding the heat in here somewhat oppressive, you may recall, Mister Ruskin.'

'Yes, quite. I find that even when I manage to get it up, it never stays up long enough for me to do anything worthwhile. I'm sure you know the feeling, do you not, Thomas?'

Well, there really isn't any answer to that, is there?

After that dreadful evening I think that you will not be surprised to learn that my friendship with the brothers of the artistic revolution began to fade away.

I still saw Rossetti with some regularity, and Hunt on occasions. But Johnnie Millais scarcely spoke a word to me after that evening at the Ruskins, for reasons that only now are becoming clear. And I never again met either John Ruskin or his poor slighted wife, Effie. And the loss is undoubtedly mine.

Will Hunt was becoming increasingly involved in matters of religion, while Rossetti was becoming increasingly involved with the beautiful Lizzie Siddal. His 'Sid', as he calls her, who lies about the place, looking ill and well by turns, while Gabriel draws and paints her with every moment of daylight.

The Academy Exhibition came and went and no windows were broken over the PRB, though there were some that sat up and took notice. And Ruskin threw his mighty weight behind them, which was a massive push for their ideals.

And Gabriel had another interest. To relieve his painful headaches and help him sleep, he had begun to experiment with all manner of pills and potions. Opium and chloral were among them, and he constantly urged me to join him. But I saw the first signs around his eyes of what was happening, and I politely refused.

During that summer of 1850, I found myself more and more at a loose end for something to occupy my time. I still lived in Seven Dials, but the urge was becoming greater and greater to go and see the world.

In the City, it would have been about June, I was nearly

caught and impressed by a gang led by a gangling young lieutenant, but I dodged away down Old Swan Lane and made my way over the mud of the foreshore, hiding for a time under the bridge until the coast was again clear.

Much as I hated the idea of impressment, there was a part of me that somehow regretted that I had escaped it. At least I would have had something to do and somewhere to go. It was a sense of futility that began to possess me. And yet the days somehow passed. There was always one of the girls in the house willing to lie an hour with me for a shilling or two.

You will wonder about the man in the cloak. I am sure that I did. There were times when I pressed Aunt Eliza as to the identity of the man, but she clammed up tighter than a ten-a-penny oyster. Once, when well into the tenth gin of the evening, she muttered something about ending up with her throat slit in the Fleet if *he* heard that she'd been blabbing off.

So I simply kept waiting, somehow feeling that one day all would be revealed.

There was one incident that summer that I will look back on for the remainder of my life with the greatest regret and sorrow. It was a little after the Summer Exhibition, and came at a time when I was at the end of my rope as to what to make of myself.

It was towards the end of a warm June.

Uncle Abe had been urging me to join him in the business, and I was close to agreeing, merely for something to do with myself. Despite the fact that I felt it would be a damnable waste of a good bit of learning.

As I recollect it, the day was a Saturday. And the sun was peering at London through the usual morning haze. Abe had asked me to aid him in carrying a small parcel for him to a jeweller friend of his who lived over the nobby side of town. Beyond the Palace, and north. Not too far from the new cricket ground at Lords, where I passed many an idle and pleasant afternoon.

I was wearing an open shirt, as the temperatures had been high for some days, and I could not bear to have anything constricting about my neck. Perhaps it came from seeing too many friends and acquaintances bid their last farewells to the world from a platform outside Newgate.

And I had tucked the small parcel, well wrapped in a sealskin overcoat, down against my chest, where I felt it would be safe from the inquiring eyes of any passing peelers. It was not light, and I suppose that it must have contained jewels to the value of several hundreds of guineas. Not that Uncle Abe would see one small part of that amount.

I walked the way that I had those few years earlier when I had gone after the nest of a common bird and found myself plucking a creature of a different colour. Strolling along the width of Piccadilly, I greeted a few young ladies of my cognisance, including a pretty little slip called Bright Betty.

She was about to go on the Burlington walk, and told me how well she had been doing over the last week or so. She was greatly given to lying, but she claimed a marquis, two earls and a viscount had enjoyed her favours in the last five nights. She was a most unusually pretty thing, with the brightest eyes in London, from whence came her name, and tight little yellow curls. She wore a print dress that emphasised her small size and made her look even younger than her twelve years.*

I left her with some regret and made my way along towards St James's Park, intending to walk up Constitution Hill and enjoy the touch of greenery. It was becoming warmer and warmer, and I loosened my shirt a further couple

---

* Sadly, Tom Goane once again shows us a side of Victorian life that many would rather pretend never existed. In this hey-day of the great Empire, many of the tens of thousands of prostitutes were children of twelve and younger.

of buttons, noticing that the cotton was wearing thin and needed replacement on most of them. Aunt Eliza's sewing woman came in on a Monday and I resolved to leave it for her.

Just as I was entering Constitution Hill, I heard a burst of cheering and looked round, wondering if one of the brave cavalrymen had been unhorsed. There were few more popular sights in all of London.

There were several carriages about and many a'horse. Before crossing over myself, I paused to admire a tantalising brace of classy biddies parading their wares. Not the queer blowen pavé thumpers that you saw around my home, but the real goods.

Off to show themselves around Hyde Park, where many were already walking, to eye out the ground for Albert's Exhibition, which was due to open in May of the following year.

> 'In Rotten Row, the toffs all go,
> Eyeing all the fillies . . .'

That's how one of the songs started. They were a fine sight, and many a man's head was turned to watch them, from lords to sweepers. Both this morning were tallish, turned out in their best habits, both wearing abominably tight trousers, with a short black skirt over for decency. Or the pretence of decency. Pert little hats, with a veil, draped coquettishly over their eyes.

I was among a group of nobs watching as they rode by. The stallion of the one nearest to us turned skittish, and his equestrienne cursed him as well as any navvy, digging at his flanks with her pointed silver spurs, kicking away with her mirrored riding boots, flailing at his quarters with a wicked little whip.

My hair was stirred on my neck by the collective gasps of passion from the nobs, and I heard one whisper to a friend,

135

'I'm damned if I wouldn't give a hundred pounds to be ridden in so cruel a manner.'

For me, I would rather have been in the saddle than under it.

It would be less than honest of me not to admit that my thoughts were still on those ladies as I stepped clean off the pavement, ready to cross over Constitution Hill and continue my bracing walk. And so I never even saw the horse and rider that were nearly on top of me.

'Ware hooves!'

'Look out there!'

Cries from all sides, including an oath from the man on the horse. Screams from ladies, and the grinding of carriage wheels grating together in collision. I dived forwards to avoid the rearing beast, seeing the irons strike fire from the road, noticing the rider having a damnable amount of trouble trying to control what seemed a hard-mouthed beast.

As I dived, so the buttons on my shirt popped, and out rolled the sealskin parcel, including enough trouble to put Uncle Abe in line for a topping and myself on the first hulk on the left on the Thames' shore.

Perhaps I might have cut and run, risking leaving the gems and facing Abe later. Not that I now feared him overmuch as I was both taller and stronger that he was. But to scarper was not in my nature, and I scampered in among the hooves, hearing the cries and hallooing rise around me, while I scooped up the bag and rammed it down the front of my trousers, nearly damaging poor John Thomas with the sharp end of an amethyst brooch.

I was lucky, escaping nearly scot-free, apart from a tear to my right knee and a deal of skin missing from both elbows.

But what of the rider?

One moment he was up there, tall and straight in the saddle, fighting the horse. Even to me, there was something familiar about his face. The smart hair, cropped and tugged down over the ears, and the crisp waistcoat. I had seen that face before.

But the next moment he was brought low. The mount was frightened by my appearance directly under its hooves, and then scared still more by the outcry of hooting from the watching crowds. And it kicked up, dropping its shoulder in the way that some beasts have. The rider had only two chances. Very small, and no chance at all.

He was unlucky, flying high in the air, the reins snapping in his hands with the force of the accident. His hat vanished into the sunny air, and he fell not a yard from me, landing on the road with a crash that seemed to shake the earth. I had been bending, adjusting my clothes around the bag of jewels, as well as my own jewel bag, when I saw and heard the poor fellow land. Smack a'top his pate he fell, and I saw that his neck seemed to bend and twist with the dreadful force of the blow.

His horse clattered off back towards St James's, and the rider lay quite still. Feet pounded all around me, and I was lifted up and helped to the edge of the road. I have never heard so much noise, with everyone shouting and calling, offering the best and worst advice.

'Lift him!'

'Lay him still!'

'Loosen his stock!'

'Poor Sir Robert!'

Sir Robert!

My oath! That was where I'd seen that face. I had just tumbled Sir Robert Peel from his horse. Sir Robert Peel. In my young life his was the name that hung on everyone's lips. There were those around Seven Dials who had blessed him for his reforming of the wicked penal laws, but he had then founded the police force that we called after him. Repealed the Corn Laws and given us cheaper food through Free Trade. Sir Robert Peel.

At least I hadn't killed him, as I saw that there was some movement from him.

'Carry him to his home in Whitehall Gardens!' called out some wise body. 'There he will be well.'

I was greatly relieved. More so than I can tell you. I waited that evening for news, and it was said that he was much recovered. It was even said that he would shortly be called to take up again the tiller of the ship of state as Prime Minister.

Three days later he died.

Among the thousands of the London poor who came and lined the streets for his funeral, watering the dusty cobbles with their tears, none wept more honestly for that marvellous man than did I, Thomas Goane.

CHAPTER TEN

Nothing of any great moment happened to me during that autumn and winter. Life went on, and somehow I passed another birthday. Lost touch almost completely with Gabriel and the others. Helped Uncle Abe and worked for Aunt Eliza for a spell as a chucker for her. But I rather think that she must of got word from the man in the black cloak, as she came to me with her feathers a'fluster, like a hen that has just 'scaped the fox, and told me that I was not to carry on in that line ever again.

And so, as time eased away from me, with those summer months of one's youth, the much-vaunted Great Exhibition travelled the road from being an absurd idea of good Prince Albert and now glittered for all to see in Hyde Park. And Uncle Abe had promised us that we would be there with the cream of society for the opening.

On May the first.

EDITORIAL NOTE: *This now brings us up to the point at which these extracts from Tom Goane's Journals began.*

The three of us made our way through the closing halls, with now only a few visitors still doggedly pursuing their money's worth on that first day. Count Jonathan Yglesias walked on the left, as befitted his position, with his swordstick swinging loosely in his hand. On his right arm walked Miss Meadows, still radiant in her green ensemble, looking much recovered from her fainting fit.

And I walked with them, on the other side of the lady, unable to cease from casting glances at Count Yglesias's cloak. With its bright scarlet lining. That great black cloak, and I wondered about the man. Our meeting had been so strange, like everything over the years concerning the man in the black cloak, and now I truly trembled on the further brink of excitement, knowing that the answer to the enigma of my life was about to be finally revealed.

'Oh, do look, Jonny. Look Tom. Are they not the sweetest things you ever did see?'

Christabel Meadows had stopped on our way out, standing transfixed in front of several cases of squirrels.

Dead squirrels.

Stuffed squirrels.

Stuffed squirrels all dressed up in tiny suits of clothes and dresses in a macabre series of *tableaux morts*, in a pretence of imitating human life.

'What do you think of it, Tom?'

Her hand was on my arm, and I remembered only too well that she was the 'friend' of my mysterious benefactor, for I now had not the least doubt that it was he.

'It is ... most unusual, Miss Meadows. The most unusual thing I have ever perceived.'

The Count sniffed. 'Say what you think, damn it! If you don't like it, then say so. I know that Victoria was delighted with it. For me, I swear that it makes me feel merely damned ill.'

I warmed to the Count.

We went on outside, where the lights glittered and twinkled, making the park seem like a fairy grotto. Count Yglesias paused on the edge of the grass, looking back at the glass palace, and then at Christabel, and finally at me. It was hard to tell, but it seemed at that moment that there was a light of amusement that gleamed for an instant in those deep-set eyes, but when I looked again they were without any trace of emotion.

'I have my carriage over the far side of the Park,' said Yglesias. 'Perhaps you would care to accompany us back to our town house, and then we can enjoy a friendly talk, man to man?'

'That would be most satisfactory, sir,' I said, my head spinning with the speed of events.

'Ah, but wait a moment. I believe we are expecting the ambassador of . . . of a certain major European power to dine with us tonight, are we not, Christabel?'

'Are we, Jonny?'

He placed his hand on her arm, and it looked for a moment as if he pinched her, hard. She certainly jumped and seemed about to say something. But changed her mind. However, as I have said, the light was uncertain in the Park, and I could not swear on the Bible to what I saw.

'I'm sure that you remember now, do you not, my dear one?'

'Yes. Of course, Jonathan. I recall it well.'

His teeth flashed as white as a bookie's welcome in the darkness. 'There. That is such a shame, Tom, that so soon after meeting we are not able to offer you the entertainment that we would wish. But there is always tomorrow. And that may be better. Yes, I believe that tomorrow will be even better for our meeting. Christabel is fatigued by this damned Exhibition, and it would be hard for my staff to lay on the proper sort of meal for such an occasion. So we will make it on the morrow.'

'Very well, sir. But where should I present myself, and at what time?'

'Good question, my boy. A very fair question. I see that your education has forced in a middling amount of brains. One small matter first. I don't think that this meeting is a fit subject for you to discuss with anyone. Do you follow me, Tom? Not with anyone.'

I remembered the condition of Uncle Abe, and I also recalled a certain accident with a grand piano. And I shuddered. Though the evening was not cold.

'Catching a chill, Tom? I do trust not.'

'No, sir. Must have been someone walking across my grave.'

He laughed, shaking his shoulders, so that the cloak moved on his tall frame, like the wings of a great black bat.

'Excellent. Very well, my boy. You will tell nobody, and you will present yourself at eight o'clock in the evening. On the morrow. At this address.'

He scribbled with a tiny pencil in a leather notepad that he withdrew from an inside pocket. It was a house in Eaton Place. The sort of address that I would have expected a man like Count Jonathan Yglesias to have. I took the note and placed it carefully in my coat, making sure in case of any accident that I had memorised it.

'Then we will expect you, Tom. It will be an interesting meeting, I think. But for now, Christabel and I bid you goodnight. Take care on your way home, Tom.'

And he bowed formally to me. I returned his bow, and took the gloved hand of Miss Meadows and pressed my lips to it, feeling her fingers hold onto mine for a moment longer than propriety dictated.

Or did it?

By this time I was so bemused that I felt that I could have imagined anything. Even imagined that I had ever met them. Perhaps they didn't really exist at all?

'Perhaps they don't really exist at all.' I was talking to myself. The street was empty, apart from a cab picking up a fare at the Belgrave Street end of Eaton Place.

I was quite befuddled. I had scarcely slept a wink the previous night, there hard under the tiles of the rookery, my mind playing on what might come to pass this next evening over dinner.

And I had even bathed. Giving Abe cause for concern.

142

'It's either a girl, or he's ill, Eliza,' he'd said. 'There's no other explanation.'

If only they knew. I had almost hugged myself with the pressure of bursting excitement inside me.

My best clothes. Nothing flash for them. And then, just after seven, I set out to walk there. There was a temptation to ride, but I knew many of the cabbies and had no wish to have my visit to Eaton Place gossiped all over London.

I had expected more or less anything. Except for what I actually found.

It was empty.

Quite, quite empty.

There were cobwebs at the windows, and dust lay thick over the sheeted furniture that I saw through the unshuttered casements around the back. It was immediately obvious that there was no point in ringing the bell, with only shadows to answer, so I climbed in over the back, and skirmished around. 'Perhaps they don't really exist at all,' I repeated to myself.

'Pssst! Come 'ere, you.'

I looked quickly round, my hand flying automatically to the knife in its snug sheath. But when I saw the owner of the voice, I let my hand relax.

'You Goane?'

'I've only just arrived,' I said, mishearing him.

'No. You Tom Goane, 'cos I got somefink for you if you are?'

It was a tramp, so dirty and overgrown with patches of green that I had not noticed him among the unweeded bushes near the kitchen door. He looked any age between nineteen and ninety, and had no teeth left in his head. Just blackened and rotting gums. He stood up, and reached no more than five feet in height.

'I'm Tom Goane. You've got a message for me?'

'Yerrsss. Give us a bob. 'E said you would.'

'Message first.' Then, 'Who? Who told you this?'

I knew the answer with a sick certainty, before he even opened his mouth.

'Geezer in a cloak. Black as your hat, it was. Give me this bit of paper to wait around 'ere and gives to you. That's what 'e said.'

'Then give it me.'

'Bob first.'

'Be hanged to you! Give it me or I'll break your damned neck like a rat in a trap.' I was not in the mood for any trifling delay.

'Damn your eyes, guv'nor. I'm an old man and I fought for King and . . .'

'The paper,' I snapped.

Hand shaking, the tramp threw me a scrap of card, so that I had to bend down for it. By the time I had straightened up, he had gone. I could hear a crashing among the bushes near the bottom of the garden, but I saw he had got away. And I cared not. All I cared for was that small piece of paper.

I carried lucifers with me, and I struck one with fingers that trembled more than I would have expected. It was a large calling card with the name 'Count Jonathan Yglesias' upon it in an ornate Gothic, golden script. The writing was on the back, in an ink of deep purple, neatly printed in a bold hand. It was short and to the point.

It said, 'Dear Tom, I fear this will come as something of a disappointment, but we have been forced to make sudden alternative arrangements. Perhaps in another time and in another place. Until then I beg you to accept my apologies and those of Christabel. Look upon this as the end of the beginning. And not as the beginning of

THE END

*   *   *

This ends the first of the Journals of Thomas Goane.